Neko The Inventive Wanderer Tales of Extraordinary Beings Book 2

Adam Thomas Applebaum

ISBN: 0-9970505-0-0
ISBN-13: 978-0-9970505-0-9

DEDICATION

This book is dedicated to my karaoke fans and friends as well as those who are fans of my novel series thus far. I hope you all live happy and fulfilled lives and continue to support my efforts to immortalize myself through the content I produce.

CONTENTS

ACKNOWLEDGMENTS

After the last book, others may be wondering since the subtitle is called "Tales of Extraordinary Beings," there must be more than one being with extraordinary characteristics. You would be right and this is one of those such beings. This timeline takes place from the Year 1990 C.E. to 2000 C.E. Neko and others in my series will not have any impact on each other's stories until series 2 even if they make special appearances in them.

My next series will be after Book 4 of this one and they will all come together. Plans are subject to change as the last two characters have fewer years to work with, and some of their backstories may work better together than as a standalone.

The following is rated 18+ for crude humor and strong sexual content in written form. You have been warned. Also new characters such as Danielle or others based on real people were used either with permission or coincidentally. For the Adam The Forsaken fans I also added a chapter for him and other potential antagonists to get a little spotlight. This is not just filler, there is a method to the madness! Additionally I'd like to thank the many people who bought the last one in the series and those who have waited for me to come up with something new for their patience and support. Further I would like to extend a special thank you to Hiroki Shima, for promoting my works internationally as he wanders the globe.

i

1 AN INVENTOR IS BORN!
A New Beginning.

Neko was a gifted blond haired blue eyed cat boy. He was born in Julian, California. Julian. California is a beautiful small town area famous for its apple pies. As a baby, he tinkered with hobby kits and made cute little toys. His mother, "Ann" and father "Thomas," were very proud of their little boy. Neko wasn't an only child. He had a brother named Caleb, who was declared from birth to be a genius. Neko had no contact at all with his brother, except during vacation periods. His brother was about 8 and a half years old when Neko was born. By this point, Caleb had earned a Bachelor's Degree in Mechanical Engineering and was working part time for an auto shop while he furthered his education at The Furlington Academy.

Caleb was a relatively quiet person and no one ever seemed to know what was going on in his head. He hadn't interacted with other children growing up so Ann and Thomas were a bit worried that Caleb was missing out on an important part of life. Their wish when Neko was born was for him to have a childhood that children were supposed to have. One with friends, social relationships, and educational enrichment.

When Neko was a baby, he didn't seem to have interest interacting with other babies. Neko was always preoccupied with tinker toys and other baby related items designed to help one's infant learn to do many things in life without overwhelming their brain. His parents were able to teach him relatively quickly, how to use a toilet. Speaking and walking were just as easy for Neko to learn. Once Neko learned to walk he was busier than ever with his toys and other forms of baby enrichment.

By the time Neko was two years old, he quickly grew bored of the toy sets his parents had bought for him. Neko was often found getting into Thomas' tool kit and making toys out of anything he could find. He was so good at what he did, his parents entered him in a Toddler Science fair for gifted toddlers. The contest allows entrants between the ages of zero and four years old to enter the competition. By this point, Neko knew how to read schematics and had an extensive vocabulary that would make even Einstein jealous.

The other contestants showcased ordinary things like bubble gum machines with paper cutout hands. The better ones had simple machines that are typical of an elementary school science fair. Neko won the event easily. He made a real working robot out of junkyard parts and put them together right before the judge's eyes. Neko said, "As you can see I have successfully soldered together a working robot designed to do anything I ask. Observe." Neko ordered the robot to fetch some coffee for the judges. It went over to a coffee machine and poured some coffee to the judges who were more than a little stunned that a toddler could speak so well let alone put together something this sophisticated. It brought the coffee to them and the judges drank some and did a rather cartoony spit take on each other.

The judges handed him the trophy for best invention and the act of science at the event. Even his own parents were impressed. Ann said, "Hmm I am really glad the stuff we gave Neko paid off but, I am a bit worried about him. What if he ends up just like his brother?" Thomas laughed and said, "Oh please! He managed to make a robot and speak well at a science fair one time. This isn't anything a middle or high school student wouldn't be able to do. While it would naturally be seen as gift at his age, it isn't quite 'Furlington Academy' material. There is still time to encourage him to be more social and slow down on the learning." That night Neko got home barely able to haul the trophy he'd just won into his room. He slept well that night knowing he had done something good.

When Neko was three years old, he was given a special invitation to join a middle school science fair. He accepted and entered that same robot into it and won at the Science Fair. His prize was an even shinier trophy, and a small sum of cash to do with as he pleased. The very next day invited to a high school science fair. Neko entered that same invention and won a full Scholarship to the Furlington Academy for Gifted Youths. News of Neko's exploits spread fast and it wasn't uncommon for him to get a visit from various news stations. During news interviews and science fairs he had to hide his hybrid features from the public as hybrids were not well known at this time. Neko was pretty much the hot topic and his parents were able to open a savings account for him so that he could collect interest on all the money he was earning for appearances in commercials, talk shows, and other media coverage.

Despite Neko's overwhelming success, Caleb didn't seem bothered by it at all. He never did care what anyone thought of him, and kept himself busy at the Furlington Academy finishing his education.

2 A NEW FRIEND
Or is she more?

When Neko turned 4 years old, his obsession with building things grew. He even went as far as to upgrade modern appliances around the house with cool features. Ann and Thomas loved their son a lot, and occasionally took him outside to play with other kids. Neko didn't seem very interested in playing with others at all. This made his parents worry. This changed slightly, when a cute little cat-girl the same age as Neko approached him. Neko was tinkering in an open area when the girl found him. She had short pink hair that barely reached her shoulders and light green eyes.

"Hello! My name is Sena!" She said in a cute but polite voice. "I am Neko" replied Neko while tinkering with his hobby kits, not even bothering to look her way. Sena smiled and turned Neko away from his portable inventing table. Neko blushed a little as he found her very attractive but, was too innocent to know what he was feeling. Sena said, "Don't you ever get tired of making toys all the time?" Neko replied, "No I love making toys." Sena asked, "Making toys is cool but, have you ever tried playing with them?" Neko said "No most of my toys play with themselves as they run on batteries and do only a certain actions. I do have a few RC vehicles, though." Sena said, "Show me!" She jumped up and down excitedly like a child begging for a cool toy.

Neko pulled out his RC cars and gave a remote control to Sena. The two of them played with their RC car happily until the sun went down. Sena's Mom named, "Alison" and Dad named "Alexander," called for her to come home as the sun came down. Sena replied "Coming Mommy and Daddy! See you tomorrow Neko!" Neko and Sena went back to their respective parents. Ann asked, "Neko did you have fun with your new friend today?" Neko replied, "Yes mommy! We had so much fun playing with our RC cars!" Thomas said, "How cute! You found yourself a playmate." Neko replied in a voice that sounded like he was embarrassed by that statement, "Dad it isn't like that!" He ate dinner with his family and went to bed until the next day.

The next day Sena came out to play with Neko again. It was about summer time when this happened so, Sena invited him over to play in her lake with her.

Neko decided it wouldn't kill him to take a day off of making toys. Neko got in a pair of swim trunks, and Sena wore her one piece. Neko said, "You look good in that Sena." Sena said, "Thanks, those swim trunks of yours are cute!" Neko was wearing swim trunks with kittens on them.

Neko went into the water and he giggled as fish were coming up to suck on his skin. Neko said, "Wow these fish seem to love me." Sena said, "Nah they are just checking to see if you are food or not. Even if they thought you were food, their teeth aren't sharp enough to hurt you. If anything, they will just nibble at your dead skin cells for whatever sustenance they provide." Neko asked, "So you have been studying fish?" Sena said, "Yes it is kind of my dream to be a Marine Biologist so, I can swim with fish and gather research on them. Perhaps I could make a few documentaries on how they live." Neko said, "That sounds like fun." Sena said, "Yeah the lab work would be but, I am only learning to read and I don't quite have the index yet to be one. It may take a while for me to get into the Furlington Academy or any college. Last I checked, no one hosts 'marine biology' competitions."

Sena continued, "To get in any other way would require a series of assessment tests on topics entirely unrelated to stuff I'd need to know to go out diving. So I haven't really bothered with it. Also congratulations on your scholarship to the Furlington Academy." Neko said, "Thanks but, I barely even remember the competition that got it for me. All of the sudden I woke up one day surrounded by trophies and awards. It is like I had done something completely stupid after getting an award, and I woke up the next day not remembering any of it." Sena asked, "do you intend to apply to the Furlington Academy?" Neko said, "I might but I have never been in school before, and I don't know what to expect." Neko asked, "How would you feel if I was suddenly sent away there?" Sena said, "I would miss you. I really do enjoy talking to you and playing like this." Neko said "Exactly. I would like to apply myself to my capabilities but, I just feel so happy when I am with you, that I don't want to leave you behind."

Sena hugged him tightly and said, "If it were up to me we'd both be there, but if only one of us can, I don't want to hold you back." Neko said "Thanks, Sena!" Neko played with Sena, laughing like a child and chasing her in the water.

Neko began pruning and got out of the water with Sena. The two of them enjoyed an ice cream cone with red velvet and chocolate chip ice cream on them. Neko and Sena went inside after enjoying their ice cream and before they knew it, the time had come for Neko to go home. Neko seemed disappointed but went to his house like a good boy. Sena hugged him goodbye. Both Neko's and Sena's parents smiled to each other seeming happy. Both families called it a night and went to bed, and both Neko and Sena dreamed of each other that night.

3 THE FURLINGTON ACADEMY
The School of Intense Knocks

The next day came and Neko went to a local junkyard to find some scrap metal to make some cool devices. Neko began building a servant robot that would fetch him food and drink whenever he commanded it to. It took him about a week of diligent work to complete it. It was his first time attempting such a feat, since he was a toddler. When his parents saw what he'd done, they fainted in shock. The next day Neko woke up to hear his parents talking in the next room.

He put his ear closer to the wall to listen in. Ann "I just don't know what to do anymore. It was cute when he was just tinkering with some toys, but now he's gone back to real machines!" Thomas said, "Well sooner or later we have to let him go. Everyone has a destiny to fulfill, and Neko is no exception." Ann replied with tears welling up in her eyes, "But, I was hoping that wouldn't happen until he was, at least, a teenager! We already have one genius in the family as it is!" Thomas said, "I know honey, we both wanted an average child to raise through the typical milestones of life but, we can't always get what we want. We need to think about what is best for him and our world."

Ann said while still crying, "You aren't seriously going to enroll him in the Furlington Academy are you? He is too young to be off on his own, and he just made a friend! How will we explain this to her?" Thomas replied, "I don't know but, it would be a crime to deny him from realizing his full potential. So, yes I will enroll him right now and someone will be by to pick him up tomorrow. They will assess his skill set at the campus. If all goes well, they'll take him." Neko burst into tears hearing everything they said. Neko said, "I-I f-failed m-mommy and d-daddy as their son." He then raised his Arclight Spanner into the air. Neko's sorrow quickly turned to determination as he declared, "I may have failed to be the son my parents wanted, but I won't fail the world as what I was destined to be. I will be the best inventor this world has ever known!" And so it came to Pass Neko was enrolled in the Furlington Academy. Sena saw Neko off and both of them were crying not wanting to be separated.

Neko began his first day in his classes and dual majored in Mechanical Engineering and Robotics.

Caleb had by this point had earned his Ph.D. and opened up his own robot shop where he customized robots for any need and any shape or size. Neko made exceptional progress and became a top student at the academy, just like his brother before him. He spent his spring break contemplating how it had all come to this on his bed. His roommate, "Bates," was a frat leader and seemed concerned for him.

Bates said, "Hey Neeks, I heard what happened." Neko looked up at him inquisitively. "What's it to you, Bates? Most people's parents would be happy to have someone qualify for this place at my age, but not mine." Bates said, "We all got problems in life man every one of us. Despite it, you've always seemed so dutiful about getting a project done, but now you got a chance to go back home for a short time and you are just going to pass it up?"

Neko replied "Yeah, but you know as well as I that my parents hate the fact I am a genius." Neko asked, "Why would I go home?" Neko continued, "If I do, it'll just be another tearful goodbye once it is over. It is not worth it to spend a week. The week will be all too brief." Bates said, "And I am sure your idea of time off of school is to sit around here feeling sorry for yourself. There are so many others out there who would kill to be you! For Pete's sake, you even have a special friend back home who is probably missing you now!" Bates asked, "Don't you want to see her again?" Neko face palmed "I can't believe I am even listening to advice from someone who spends his days goofing off with a fraternity, and thinks a siphon drum pump and beer is living the life! But, I concede you do make a solid point. I have been curious to know what Sena has been up to."

Bates sighed and said, "Now you are bringing me down and all I am trying to do is help you! It seems in your vastly intelligent mind, you've not learned that those around you have feelings too." Neko replied "I am well aware that others have feelings. However, I don't see a reason not to tell it like it is. People have a right to know the truth." Bates said, "You know, I think that's one trait I've come to appreciate most about you. I mean, I may not like the truth but, in this world, it is refreshing to have someone who can be honest about how I come off. It is never a mystery what you think of me." Neko said "I am glad you feel this way. Well, 'Master Bates,' I'll go on one condition." Bates asked, "What is that?"

Neko said, "As long as you don't completely trash the room with your parties while I am away I will return home to see my loved ones." Bates said, "You can count on me Neko Neko Bo Beko Beko Ta Teko Teko Fe Fi Fo Feko!"

4 SPRING BREAK
7 Days of Fun in the Sun!

Neko packed his bags and went home. When Neko got home not much had changed. The same people he'd grown up with got a bit older but otherwise, it was the same old small town he'd loved since he left not more than three months. Sena was wandering the town, getting some groceries for her mom and dad like a good girl. It was at that time she found Neko with his bags.

Sena said, "Neko! I am so happy to see you!" Neko replied, "Hi Sena, it has been awhile and I am sorry I never called you or visited until now." She tackled him with a hug and held onto him. Sena said, "While you were away I asked your parents where you went. They told me you went to the 'Furlington Academy.'" Neko sighed and said, "Yes I did, they didn't even ask me first and I overheard them crying over the fact they didn't get to raise a 'normal' child. I am ever so glad to know they wanted a complete collection by having a genius, an average, and probably next on the list was a dumbass!" Sena hugged him crying tears of both loneliness and sympathy because she'd missed not getting to see him for over a month. Sena said, "Neko… come home with me! You don't have to be in a house with a family that doesn't love you!"

Something inside Neko compelled him to go with her. He'd still not yet grasped it, as he was not exactly in touch with his own emotions. Neko said, "Alright I will stay with you for this week then. As much as I'd hate to be a burden on you, I am not ready to face my family after their rash decision to send me away without even asking me how 'I' felt about it."

.With that Neko went to Sena's Cottage near the lake and met her mom and dad. Alison said, "Aww what a cute cat-boy!" She snuggled Neko tightly who purred loudly and blushed with embarrassment. Since his parents hadn't snuggled him as much during the times he was inventing things, he was putty in her hands.

Alexander said, "Aww did his parents never give him any affection?" Sena explained the situation as best she could to her parents. Alison said, "Poor thing, sounds like he needs some delicious apple pie with ice cream and whipped cream on it.

Neko's eyes lit up and said, "As much as the Furlington Academy has, they cannot hold a candle to the apple pie baked up here by apples grown right from our trees. With the beep of an oven, the apple pie was ready.

Alison pulled it out of the oven and served it for her family and Neko. Sena began eating some happily with Neko. Every so often the two exchanged looks at each other and blushed.

Alison whispered, "Ahh young love isn't it beautiful?" Alexander whispered "It sure is honey, I wonder how long it will take for them to realize it." Alison whispered, "Sena seems to be catching on, but Neko, as smart as he is, seems emotionally oblivious to it."

Neko didn't appear to know how to take what he'd heard them saying, as cats have exceptionally good hearing. Sena blushed and asked, "Neko after this pie, would you like to play with me in my room?" Neko shrugged and said, "I don't see why not." After the meal was complete Sena excitedly showed Neko to her room which was chock full of plush toys and stuff typical of a rural girl's room in the 1990s.

Neko said, "I see you take exceptionally good care of your toys and what not." Sena said, "Come on the bed please and let's play." Neko at this point had been to what is by anyone's definition a college so, he unlike other boys his age might confuse what is usually an innocent invitation to play with toys on a comfortable surface, as sexual innuendo. Neko blushed and said, "O-Ok..." He got on the bed with her and she snuggled him tightly. A plushy of Adam The Forsaken from Book 1 of this series, was the only thing symbolically separating the two from direct contact.

Neko looked at the doll closely. Neko said, "Hmm, that toy seems so sad, but why?" Sena said, "I made it myself when I stopped getting to see you. I saw what appeared to be a miserable looking human in Covina Park. My parents took me on a trip there a few months ago.. They told me, I had to hide my tail and ears while visiting Covina. Weirder still, the boy I saw playing by himself in the park didn't smell human at all, but no one else seemed to notice. All I know is something very unusual is going on. All that aside, I modeled this doll to represent how he seemed to feel because, I too felt it when you were gone.

Neko suddenly felt something happen in his chest and without warning he set the Adam doll aside and hugged Sena gently. Sena seemed to enjoy the embrace a lot. Sena asked, "Neko are you feeling ok?" Neko said, "I don't know my rational mind cannot comprehend what it is I am feeling right now. I feel an urge to hang onto you."

Sena laughed and said, "Aww the genius doesn't know what emotions are?" Neko said, "I know what they are, but this is my first time actually feeling any kind of connection to another person. I don't even know what to call it." Sena blushed and said, "Its ok Neko. This may be an awkward time to mention this, but we don't exactly have a guest bed. My bed is big enough for two so, it shouldn't be a problem." Neko blushed again realizing that she may be too innocent to know just what she is implying. Sena yawned a bit and fell asleep. She held Neko tightly and did not want to let him go. Neko felt a bit uneasy at first, but eventually settled down in her warm embrace.

The next day came and both Sena and Neko woke up with a yawn. Neko would not have to return to the Furlington Academy for another 6 days. Sena said, "Hey Neko, my parents rented a movie for us if you want to watch it." Neko asked, "What is a movie?" Sena laughed hysterically and said "Seriously Neko? All you ever did was your school work at that Academy?" Neko said, "Yeah that's pretty much all I had time for if I wanted to be at the top of the class." Sena said, "Wow everyone there must be incredibly smart!"

Neko said, "Yeah most are but, that doesn't stop them from doing stupid things just because they can. Why just last week a chemistry student got drunk, lit a fart on fire, and had to be sent to a hospital." Sena said, "Geeze! Standards there must be strict, if students got to get drunk to keep their sanity." Neko said, "Yeah for some maybe, I mean the college is almost all made up of child prodigies. Prodigies are rare and hybrids and furries are as well. That place can't very well stay in business, if they don't occasionally accept a few regular people of typical college age. Unless they raised tuition like crazy."

Sena asked, "Um is everyone there a hybrid?" Neko said, "No, currently there are efforts to integrate us and colonize the planet or so I've heard their staff murmur. However, some places are better prepared to accept us than others." Sena said, "Well that explains why that human that didn't smell human, but looked it. He was probably hiding his animal features."

Neko said "Yeah places like Julian don't really care about trivial matters as race as they depend on tourism a lot. Places like Covina apparently don't share the same sensibilities I take it. In fact, I'd bet most of the humans here think we are just cosplaying."

Sena said, "Well in fairness this place isn't on a state map so, more often than not, people come here by accident." Sena inserted a VHS into the VCR. I doubt most people remember using these days. The video was a performance of "Cats." "Cats," is a classic theatre performance. Neko said, "I don't know if I should be insulted, or flattered that those humans dressed up as cats." Sena replied, "Well on the bright side, this might explain why some people around here don't seem to notice we aren't human, or if they do they don't care." They continued watching it till it was over. Neko said, "Alright for what it's worth, it did have some enjoyable music and events going on in it. However, I feel like I watched the cat hybrid equivalent to a Minstrel show."

The author would like to apologize to any people of African or South American or Central American descent, if that line was in any way offensive.

Sena said, "I am surprised you know what one is given you'd never even seen a movie." Neko said, "We went over it in Ethnic Studies class, which is a curriculum requirement among others." Sena sighed and said,"Well then what should we do now? we still got the whole afternoon ahead of us." Alexander and Alison came into the room. Alexander asked, "Sena, Neko, will you two be ok on your own?"

Neko said, "Sure!" Sena asked, "Why?" Alison said, "Because your father and I need to go to work. We do not get this day off as you guys do." Sena said, "Sure mommy we'll be fine!" They left for work, with that all said and done. Sena sniffed herself and said, "Whew, it smells like I need to shower, see you in a few Neko."

She went to the bathroom, leaving Neko to his own devices. She unconsciously forgot to lock the door. Neko thought to himself, "Sena sure is cute. What I wouldn't give to help her get into the Furlington Academy. If I do, I would have another distraction from my career." He heard Sena sing from the shower in the most beautiful voice he'd ever heard and his heart began to thump.

Neko thought to himself, "Is this what my parents called love? Could they have been right all along? But, I can't tell Sena there is no way she wouldn't be disgusted at the notion I could love her... I cannot live without her... but I cannot tell her..."

Meanwhile, in the shower, Sena thought to herself, "I feel so happy and funny in my tummy when I am near him. My mommy said that when you feel that sensation you are in love, but is he ready for it? Could this be real? We are still young so, how could it be? Hmmm, I found a weird substance in daddy's dresser the other day. I wonder what it does."

Neko had to use the bathroom at that moment, but the nearest bathroom was the one Sena was in. He couldn't find the other bathrooms. Neko knocked on the door a little harder than he intended and it swung open. Sena was behind a shower curtain and the shower was going so loud she didn't hear him. Neko opened his pants to take a piss and accidentally flushed the toilet, not knowing what it would do if someone happened to be showering.

Sena felt the water get hot and jumped out naked into Neko's arms. She screamed in pain from the hot water and embarrassment that she was naked in front of Neko. Neko got knocked to the ground and he slid into a wall and hit his head. He was out cold. Sena finished showering and got dressed pulled up Neko's pants and lay him on the couch.

Sena thought to herself, "Oh no I hurt him... worse still he saw my most private of parts..." Neko finally came to and said, "S-Sena I am sorry, I didn't know that if I flushed the toilet, it would make the water that hot!" I just had to pee urgently and was hoping I could just piss and go. I didn't mean to..." Sena said, "N-No I-I am sorry for knocking you out cold..." Neko said, "If there is anything I can do to make this up to you just name it I'll do it!" Sena said "Well um... I am kind of tense and sometimes my daddy rubs lotion into my hands and feet. I find it relaxing you know..." Neko nodded and ran to the bathroom and found the pomegranate cream from under the sink and brought it in. Sena pulled off her socks and shoes revealing her cat hind paws to him.

Both of them looked into each other's eyes laughing awkwardly as Neko began rubbing her back legs with the lotion and felt her soft, delicate paw pads. She started laughing out of control because, he wasn't rubbing hard enough. Neko rubbed a bit firmer so it wouldn't tickle anymore. He could hear her breathe a sigh of relief once he increased the pressure a bit.

Sena asked nervously, "N-Neko?" Neko asked, "Yes Sena?" Sena asked, "If I tell you something anything, will you promise you won't hate me?" Neko said, "Sure, I've heard some pretty strange stuff at the Furlington Academy so, go ahead." Sena said "Well when I am with you I feel different. Like when I am in your midst I feel so happy, but when you are gone I am so sad." Neko said, "Yeah it is part of the reason, I won't go back to my parents. I can't go back until I become a success like my older brother. Then, they will be sorry they didn't love me." He didn't realize he'd begun rubbing her feet harder, until he heard a joint in her feet pop.

Neko said, "S-Sena did I just hurt you?" Sena replied, "No I was just a bit stiff there, thanks but it probably wouldn't kill you to ease up a bit." Neko said, "Sorry, I never realized that when discussing painful topics, I'd have a tendency to manhandle things." She smiled and said, "Neko, I have something to confess to you." Neko said "I do too but um, do you promise you won't hate me if I tell you?" Sena said, "I won't hate you I promise!" Neko said, "I-I L-Love you! Mew!" he said blushing a dark red. Sena responded, "I was going to say the same, Mew!"

The two of them hugged each other tightly. Sena's Tail and Neko's tail swayed happily and touched to form a single heart. The two exchanged a kiss for the first time their bodies were vibrating more than ever and Neko got a natural bulge out of excitement rather than anything sexual. Both Neko's and Sena's cat ears flicked in different directions. They held each other's hands and stared into each other's eyes and time seemed to slow down just for them.

Neko and Sena were purring uncontrollably in each other's embrace. Sena said, "N-Neko?" Neko said, "Y-yes?" Sena said, "I found something strange in my parents' room." She pulled out a bag of catnip and showed it to Neko. Neko said, "Hmm that is some weird stuff. Looks kind of like the stuff I've seen frat boys smoke on campus but it says catnip on the label." Sena said, "I heard it lowers inhibitions if smoked or sniffed, whatever that means." Neko said, "Hmm sounds like it is soothing then."

Neko pulled out a wooden smoking pipe that looks like one Sherlock Holms would smoke. He put it in his mouth and said, "Elementary, my dear Watson!"

Sena laughed at his attempt to imitate one of the most famous fictional detectives in the world. Neko said, "Well I suppose the only way to find out what the catnip actually does, is to test it." Neko opened the catnip bag and put some into the catnip pipe, closed the bag and went to the kitchen to light it up with the stovetop. Once lit the scent of it filled the air. Neko brought the catnip pipe back to Sena's bedroom. Sena said, "Wow that smells good." Her body began squirming under the smell of it because, she is a cat person. Neko took a puff of it and began squirming like Sena because, he is also a cat person. Neko said, "I feel strange, my body it's rubbing itself on stuff, this is so weird!" Sena said, "Me too!" The catnip pipe puttered out after about fifteen minutes.

After such they had control of themselves again. However, they were still under its side effects which include lack of inhibitions and inability to deny how they truly feel. Neko said, "S-Sena I-I can't keep this to myself anymore. Blame the catnip for it but, when I accidentally saw you come out of the shower, I felt really excited in a way I'd not before." Sena smiled and said, "I kind of liked that you came in like that, and I was kind of hoping you would have come in with me. Then you startled me so, I did what I would if this were a horror movie and a killer was about to get me." Neko said, "Well if that is the case, um." Sena looked at him puzzled. Neko said, "well, despite being in an Academy, I've never until today seen a female body so could we explore each other?" He had the darkest blush on his face as did Sena.

Sena said, "I-I suppose. Where should we start?" Neko said, "Well, I guess we can begin with our belly buttons?" He pulled up his shirt only enough to show his belly button and Sena rubbed it gently listening with awe, as he purred like a kitten and relaxed. Sena said, "You are so cute Neko!" Neko blushed purring more at the response. Neko pulled up Sena's shirt just enough to show her belly button and began rubbing it listening to her purr loudly like a kitten.

Sena asked, "Now what?" Neko said, "Well I guess we could take our shirts off." Sena blushed redder "You want to see my nipples?" Neko nodded blushing more. She took it off and Neko took off his shirt. Sena covered her nipples with her hands, feeling a little embarrassed. Neko smiled blushing a lot his bulge in his pants becoming more noticeable. Sena said, "I feel very strange." Neko said "Me too, my pants feel too tight."

Neko's tail wrapped around Sena's and she uncovered her nipples. Neko said "They are really nice. Can I touch?" Sena nodded looking the other way. Neko gently poked her nipples and ran his fingers along them watching with intrigue, as they seemed to pop out and get harder. She let out a cute mew and purred with pleasure as he did so.

Sena said, "N-Neko...I-I don't know what I am feeling but, I like it!" Neko replied, "I-I am uncomfortable in my pants, I can't bear to wear them anymore." He blushed and removed his pants he was wearing boxers with cute kittens on them that said "Mew" in every known language. Sena took off her shorts and she had Panties with Neko's face on them. Neko blushed a lot. Neko asked, "Um Sena did you make these as well?"

Sena nodded and said, "Yeah I missed you so much while you were at the Furlington Academy. When I wasn't swimming underwater looking at fish, I took up sewing with my mom as a hobby. She taught me how to embroider images onto fabrics and I asked your parents for a picture of you so I could practice embroidery and they were happy to give one. I then pin pricked the image into the underwear, until it formed an exact match of your likeness and sewed together the panties when I was done."

Neko was blushing redder at the idea of his face on her unmentionables. Sena continued, "I wasn't sure how you'd react, so when you came into the bathroom and saw me naked that you'd think it creepy if you happened to find them. That and, well I was a little embarrassed to be seen naked too. In retrospect, I think the fact that I put your face on my unmentionables before I knew you loved me is a little more embarrassing." She blushed heavily after confessing all that.

Suddenly they both heard footsteps and a turning of a key in the front door. The front door opened and Alexander shouted, "Sena! Neko! We are home!" Alison skipped up the stairs and opened the door to find the two in their underwear. Neko said, "It's not what it looks like I swear!" Sena said, "Mommy?!" Alison laughed and said, "It is ok kids it is healthy for children your age to be curious about what makes you a boy and a girl." Neko said "Really?" Alison said, "Yeah enjoy your underwear party kids" she giggled as she closed the door and went downstairs. Alexander asked, "What was that all about?" Alison said, "Oh nothing, the kids were just playing doctor."

Neko blushed heavily and was moaning in pleasure and pain. The first time a male experiences ejaculation, is a bit painful like a toothpick going through one's pee hole. The semen was warm and if one were to look at them under a microscope, they'd be trying to find her womb." Sena said with a rather fiendish grin, "Drink your milk kitten!" Neko shook his head. Sena put her ears back and growled: She said sternly, "I wasn't asking!" Neko slowly licked up his own semen tears in his eyes. Anyone who looked into Sena's eyes could see her pupils were dilated, indicating she was still under the influence of the catnip they'd burned earlier. Sena said, "That's better! Now lick it!" She pointed to her vaginal slit. Neko did as commanded and she lay back moaning in pleasure and purring like a kitty."

He continued licking her slit cutely enjoying the taste of it. The slit was a leaking a fluid, that tasted sweeter than candy. Neko was finally enjoying this a bit and Sena couldn't take much more of it. Clear fluids burst from her slit into his mouth and down his throat. She was moaning in pleasure. Sena said, "V-Very G-Good…" Neko said, "T-Thanks…" Neko stuck his penis into her vaginal slit blood began to spill as he penetrated her with his catlike penis as she'd never had one up there and her hymen was being broken into. Sena said, "N-Neko it hurts…"

Neko's Pupils were dilated at this point the side effects of the catnip fully in swing now. Neko said, "This won't hurt for long I promise." He rammed his barbed kitty penis in and out of her repeatedly and unrelentingly. The two of them exchanged moans as it felt as though thousands of needles were scraping the walls of Sena's vaginal slit. Sena clenched her teeth from the pain and pleasure and her tail gave Neko's the death grip. He'd broken her hymen and she let out a moan of pain and pleasure that was louder than the rest. It was so loud, the parents could hear it downstairs. At that moment, the Pizza Guy came by with their Pizza. The transaction was completed and Alison yelled, "Kids! Dinner is here! Hurry up and finish your exploration of the jungle brambles so, we can eat!" The pizza guy drove off not giving the sounds upstairs a second thought.

Neko said, "Sena you are so tight I can't hold it much longer!" Sena said, "Let it go Neko it is ok!" Both Sena and Neko let their fluids loose at the same time and collapsed on the bed panting.

They slowly picked themselves up, got dressed, and went downstairs for dinner. Alexander said, "Man you two smell like you did a bit more than exploration up there." Alison said, "Well from the sounds and the smell, they probably had sex for the first time." Alexander said, "Oh dear I am going to have to hide my stash of catnip better. Just then the catnip's effects wore off. Neko asked in a panic, "What did we just do?" Sena said, "I don't know Neko but I feel so dirty." Alison said, "Apparently you both got into your daddy's catnip. It is an aphrodisiac of sorts used to spice up marriages and what not. Suffice it to say, you both got really horny for each other because of a medicinal substance. However, like alcohol it feeds on already existing feelings and lowers your impulse control to zero. Basically, if you two didn't love each other, it wouldn't have made you have sex with each other but instead, you both would have relieved yourself in separate rooms."

Alexander said, "Listen we need to keep this a secret from Neko's parents. They are already distressed enough that their boy was intellectually a genius as it is and they'd be more than a little miffed to find out he abused drugs and possibly impregnated a cat-girl at his age. Not to worry though if a child is made, we'll take care of it for you until you both come of age. Since I kept it within reach of you guys, I need to take responsibility for this." The others nodded in agreement.

Neko spent the rest of that vacation fishing with Sena and going to arcades and other places of fun until Spring Break ended. Neko had won a few plush toys for Sena making her a euphoric cat-girl and Sena promised to write to Neko and occasionally send gifts to him while he was in the Academy.

5 A FATED MEETING
A Job Offer for the sibling.

Neko returned to the Furlington Academy and resumed his studies as usual. Bates continued being the party animal as usual and Caleb got an offer with a group calling themselves The B.D.S.M. Empire. B.D.S.M. in this context isn't the same as the fetish. It spells out Bad Dudes Success Machine but, we'll use the acronym for comedy purposes from this point on.

Emperor Destroy Yu came into Caleb's Workshop. Caleb said, "What can I do you for?" Emperor Destroy Yu said, "I run a small organization that is interested in creating the latest and greatest machines. I heard somewhere that you are a very talented individual and I would like to enlist your help. I would be willing to pay you enough money to retire at 30, if you help us and even give you enough shares in companies we are sure will pay out big. Your retirement will be a comfortable one for sure. Caleb raised an eyebrow at the suspiciously good offer. Emperor Destroy Yu said, "I know what you are thinking but, really I do have lots of money to pay. Further, I understand that Julian and other small towns like it are some of the few places where humans know hybrids or furry creatures exist. Knowing this your prospects of getting rich are slim to none as long as Hybrids and Furries remain undocumented in the mainstream world, and maintain but small colonies established decades ago. If you were to try and go solo and get rich, Area 51 and the Center for Disease Control would be all over you. Knowing that you face this challenge, I want to hire you on in secret so you can get the money you deserve for your unique talents and not be taken in by the Government.

Caleb said, "You do make a good point. As long as Hybrids and Furries aren't public knowledge and hidden in small pocket colonies like this, it would be hard for me to make it big, and all my talent would go to waste. It would be a crying shame to say the least."

Caleb signed on the dotted line and went with him to a secret base inside a T-34 tank. Caleb said, " Um no offense sir but, doesn't it seem a bit odd you'd be coming in and out of here in a tank of all things?"

Emperor Destroy Yu said, "Normally it would, but I am part of a military research team for the United States. We are a secret unit called the "NMR&DA or National Military Research & Development Association. While civilians may question us, the army can confirm our validity. We test and develop war machines for the country and refurbish old models that are still effective. We are working to help the effort of Operation Desert Storm. Although things are calming down there somewhat, we can never be too careful."

Caleb said, "I see well that explains why you'd want my help. I am not one for war but, there isn't a lot of demand for my services in Julian." Emperor Destroy Yu took his tank to Carlsbad where a military-style ship was waiting to take them all the way to Alcatraz Island. Long Story short Caleb reached a place called Alcatraz Island. Caleb asked "Um isn't this where dangerous criminals used to be kept in prison? It doesn't look like any military base I've ever seen." Emperor Destroy Yu said, "Exactly because we are a secret unit in the military, they gave us a secret lab underground on this base that civilian tourists aren't allowed to see." Caleb said, "If you say so." Some other military personnel in matching outfits greeted them and Caleb was given some schematics for models they were currently developing. Caleb looked at them and said, "Wow for a secret military organization these models certainly seem dated." Emperor Destroy Yu said, "Yeah this is kind of why we needed your help." With that, Caleb began upgrading and developing new machines for the BDSM Empire under the assumed name of The NMR&DA or National Military Research & Development Association.

6 IN MEMORY, CONTROL
The Plot Thickens!

After rigorous studies and taking almost inhuman amounts of classes; Neko was able to earn his Associates' Degree at Age 6, His Bachelor's Degree at Age 8, and his Master's Degree at Age 10. The summer after Neko had earned his Master's Degree, he submitted his thesis for his Ph.D. in his dual Majors and it was under submission. If it were to be accepted, then he would have had all the Degrees he could earn in a lifetime. To celebrate his progress, he decided to go back home and tell his Parents and Sena the good news.

Meanwhile, Emperor Destroy Yu was up to no good. Emperor Destroy Yu said, "Good work all these years, Caleb. I have a new job for you but, it requires you to relocate." Caleb said, "Alright where to?" Emperor Destroy Yu said, "There is a bit of a situation in our hideout in Death Valley. We were doing some experiments with some desert wildlife there and well, our experiments worked too well to be controlled. We need you to get down there with some of your machines you made for us and take care of it."

Caleb said, "Oh you mean those experimental Infantry bots? I am not sure they are ready for something this huge. I am still testing them against security breaches." Emperor Destroy Yu said, "I am sure they will work fine. Just go out and help ok? Remember, you are under contract. If you don't do as I order, I will turn you in to Area 51!" Caleb said, "Fine I'll do it." Caleb got into a private airplane and headed for the "Death Valley" desert. Caleb was surrounded by armed guards with hidden cameras so Emperor Destroy Yu could always monitor him and ensure he complied. When Caleb arrived, he saw giant scorpion monsters. Caleb said, "Sheesh what in the name of science were you people thinking?"

Meanwhile, General Guillotine was reporting back to Emperor Destroy Yu. General Guillotine said, "Destroy Yu sir, Caleb is at the location. Our scouts reported something we've overlooked."

Emperor Destroy Yu said, "What is that?" General Guillotine said, "Well Caleb has a little brother who has shown as much or more promise than him. It is hard enough keeping our true purpose concealed from Caleb, but if we do try anything he will surely step in and try and stop us."

Emperor Destroy Yu said, "Hmm that could be a problem especially if we wish to rule the world. We have enough of a headache to worry about staying under the radar of the FBI as it is.

If we are going to overthrow the world, we have to be tactical. With the Internet around, it is becoming increasingly difficult to lie to people without being found out." General Guillotine said, "Sir Lieutenant Laser is waiting for your orders."

Emperor Destroy Yu said, "Tell him to send his men to seize this, 'brother of Caleb.' But, be careful or we'll be found out. We are not yet ready to face the entire military."

Meanwhile, Neko was walking outside of the campus which was inside a hidden forest thicket so as not to be easily discoverable by entities that would take in hybrids and furries for experimentation or whatever happens at Area 51. Suddenly a laughing gas bomb was thrown at Neko, and caused him to laugh himself out cold. A band of Ninjas carried Neko away to Lieutenant Laser. Lieutenant Laser then took him away to Emperor Destroy Yu's central lab in Alcatraz Island. Emperor Destroy Yu thanked them and rushed Neko into the mind submission chamber.

Emperor Destroy Yu said, "Ah how nice to see our little friend in one of my first inventions ever." Lieutenant Laser asked, "You actually built this?" Emperor Destroy Yu said, "Yes I did and the tank I used to bring Caleb here as well. I needed something that would allow me to control powerful entities through their memories. It was something I was developing while Caleb was making electronic fighting units so in case he turned on me we could get him to forget who he is and thus be of no harm to us anymore, while we slowly trick him into helping us from the shadows. Fortunately, after intensive testing, I figured out a way to erase memories that have nothing to do with their line of work so, they can still serve us and not be mindless zombies."

General Guillotine asked, "So, we need to remove his memories why? He knows nothing about us at all!"

Emperor Destroy Yu said, "Because, we need both of the brothers expertise in technology to rule this planet. If the two ever find out they are both working for us, it could cause sibling rivalry which would not be conducive to our plans."

Emperor Destroy Yu said, "Worse still they'll be onto our plan as one will likely find it suspicious that we've employed them both under the same secret unit of the military, when the talent would theoretically be more efficient spread out. Simply put, they will share knowledge of how things work here and if word somehow leaks to either of them what we are really after, we will have to deal with both of them at once. One will be hard enough to manage without the other."

Emperor Destroy Yu continued, "This is why we must erase Neko's memories so, he can work for us without knowing he has a family or anyone. That is if the data our scouts collected on Neko can be trusted." Emperor Destroy Yu turned on the machine and slowly but surely Neko's memories were being extracted and filtered. The retrieved memories were printed out on a page of copying paper.

The computer voice said, "Memory extraction complete." The chamber opened up. Neko came too and freaked out at what he saw in the lab. Neko yelled, "Where am I? How did I get here?" Emperor Destroy Yu said, "You were brought here to help us with a few projects as you are very skilled at making things work for you." Neko said, "Yeah I am but, I swear I must have had a life outside this lab but, for the life of me I cannot remember anything."

Emperor Destroy Yu said, "Listen here, you will build for us lots of military machines and you will make us more powerful than anything ever was. We are even prepared to make it worth your while." Neko said, "No, machines aren't supposed to be used this way. They have a much grander purpose than to wage war. I may not remember anyone or how I came to be but, I still remember my beliefs on how these things should be used and last I checked this wasn't one of them!" It was at that moment his robots he'd made for class blew a hole in one of the walls and gave him an exit. Neko ran for his life.

General Guillotine said, "Uh boss shouldn't we go after him?" Emperor Destroy Yu said, "Let him go with no memories of where he was going or who his loved ones are he poses no threat to us. Besides if he tried to tell anyone outside this facility about us they will either laugh at him or try to take him in as an alien. Besides, Caleb should be back any minute and if worse comes to worse, we can trick the two into eliminating each other so we ultimately get the best one of the two to serve us by force."

Neko thought to himself, "If I had any recollection of my life at all would I have given my machines a command to take me home?" He found a control panel on one of his robots with a home key button on it. Neko pressed the button and the robot picked him up and flew him to Julian California. Neko was right outside Sena's house. Neko thought, "So that is what this did."

An eager Sena ran outside to hug him. Her pink hair was now longer than before and hung down to her tail. Her green eyes were open wide and apparently glad to see Neko again. Sena said, "Neko I missed you so much! I am so happy that you are back!" Neko said, "Who is Neko? Who are you? You seem familiar but, I cannot quite place it." Sena teared up a little and asked, "How could you forget me, after all, we've done together as kids?" Neko said, "I really don't know. I woke up in this strange lab and have no memory of anything before then except what was learned in school, and how my skills should be used. I am not trying to hurt you, please don't cry!"

Sena cleared her throat, regained her composure and said, "Hmm... sounds like you got abducted by someone with highly sophisticated technologies perhaps even beyond this time period. Caleb hasn't been in his robot shop in six years now and locals reported that they saw an unidentified tank come through here the night he disappeared."

Sena continued, "Despite it, no one's been able to find him since we are off the grid and thus, cannot receive help from the sources as readily as others. So it doesn't surprise me the least that you might have been taken too. In the meantime, I don't want you doing anything that can get yourself killed so, please stay with me and calm yourself from the ordeal, hard as it may be." Neko sighed and said, "You are so right, catgirl who seems familiar. Stressing over it won't help me at all. After all, they didn't try to stop me from leaving so, whatever they had in mind they clearly didn't need me that badly."

7 SUMMER VACATION
The Debauchery Goes On!

Sena said, "I am Sena and well we were really close friends back in the day. You went to a place called the "Furlington Academy" and would sometimes on breaks come out to play with me but it was never anything too serious." Neko laughed and said, "'Furlington Academy.' That is a funny name for a school. It sounds so made up." Sena said, "Well like it or not it is the truth." Neko said, "Where are your parents?" Sena said, "They were called in for some private business about a week ago, and haven't returned." Neko said, "Well friend or not, I suppose I should help you somehow." He spotted a Lake near her cottage and saw a fish jump up. Neko spotted it and got an idea. Sena said, "Going fishing there, Neko?" Neko said, "Sure thing Sena!" He removed all of his clothes and jumped into the lake his predatory cat instincts took over. Sena laughed and smiled watching her longtime childhood crush hunt for food. Neko said, "Hey Sena C'mon in the water feels great!" Sena replied, "I don't have a swimsuit!" Neko asked, "What is a swimsuit?" Sena said, "Something you wear over your private parts while swimming in bodies of water for decency." Neko said, "I don't see anyone else here but, 'suit' yourself!" Sena thought to herself, "How is it after all these years and that one time when we were little, I am so shy about being naked with him?" He came out naked holding some fish in front of his crotch. Sena said, "Wow those are some nice catches, bring them into the freezer please." Neko said "Sure thing." He brought the fish into the freezer as she asked." He then went back outside and went swimming. After gathering up all the courage she could muster, Sena came outside and took off her shirt and shorts.

Neko and Sena were older now so, Sena was beginning to develop breasts and had a B cup. She was on the shorter end of that spectrum given her age. Sena was wearing a bra and panties with Neko's Face on them. She unhooked her bra which, was held together by a Velcro strip on the back so when removed it almost sounded like she ripped her bra off with how fast she pulled it off. Sena pulled down her panties and one could see that Sena was beginning to get a bit of hair down there.

She jumped in with Neko her skin and had goosebumps from both nervousness and the sudden change in temperature. This caused her nipples to be fully erect and bumpy as well. Neko eyed her glorious oval shaped breasts as she swam with him his kitty penis got erect and by this point in time was about 6 inches in length.

Sena giggled and said, "My looks like it's grown over the years." Neko blushed a little. Neko said, "I don't remember why but, every part of me is telling me you were someone, I loved heartily for a long time." Sena said, "Well Neko, we did kind of have sex when we were little under the influence of some catnip. I hit puberty relatively recently and ever since I've been craving it so badly." Neko said, "Sena I believe you. I may not remember what you described but, stranger things have happened. Show me what I must do."

She smiled and took his hands and rubbed them on her breasts from top to bottom letting out meows of pleasure as she made him rub them and this seemed to excite Neko a lot. Neko said, "These ovals are so soft, I could rub them all day." Sena blushed cutely and her tail wrapped around Neko's tail and she lowered her head. Her green eyes had hearts in them her pink colored ears twitched slightly. As if commanded by instinct, Neko leaned over and sucked on her ears.

She rubbed her body against his until his barbed kitty penis entered her vaginal slit. Both of them waded in the water moving up and down with each thrust Sena's breasts bouncing heavily as she got penetrated for the second time in her life. Neko said, "I don't think I've felt this good in a while." Sena said, "You are bigger than before but no less rough than I remember!" He began penetrating her faster and deeper her slit, gave his smaller of two heads a big hug. The two of them felt completely in sync with one another and bonded on a higher level than before. The heat of their sexual intercourse was such, that the cold water seemed lukewarm to them.

Sena felt as though a sheathed dagger was being placed into a scabbard, which was placed in front of her crotch instead of at the side where it is supposed to be. While moving it would consequently stick her in the privates. Sena said, "N-Neko I-I am going to burst! It's too big!" Neko said, "I feel like something other than piss is about to come out! I cannot hold on much longer!" Neko let loose his sperm within Sena's vaginal slit. Neko quickly swam with Sena back to shore, got dressed and went to bed.

8 THE QUEST FOR NEKO'S MEMORIES
Cats Are From Outer Space?

When Neko and Sena woke up the following day, her parents were still away. Neko said, "I am a little concerned, you said your parents left on important business a week ago. I'd think they'd have come home by now." Sena said, "Well um…I don't really know, they wouldn't tell me where they were going." Neko said, "Hmm that is unusual moreover I still feel a lot for you but I cannot remember why. It is kind of bothering me a bit." Sena said, "I don't know if it will help much but, I know where you lived when you had your memories. It might be a good place to start."

Neko said, "Very well show me to it." Sena nodded and lead him home. Thomas and Ann saw him and ran out of the house. Ann said, "Neko you are home at last!" Thomas said, "Why haven't you called or visited all these years?" Neko said, "I don't remember." Sena said, " Well not to rehash any hard feelings, but you two did make him feel pretty unwanted when you sent him away in the first place. More importantly, he doesn't remember his past at all. All he knows is what he is good at. We were hoping we could unlock a few memories that were deleted by coming here." Ann said, "Hmm sounds unusual indeed."

Thomas said, "This is merely speculation but, your brother before you disappeared 6 years ago and hasn't been found. Whatever took your memories might have also claimed him." Sena said, "Maybe so given that would make the fact that both are incredibly gifted the pattern that would explain the strange happenings. Sena said, "On that note did my parents happen to stop by before they left a week ago?" Thomas looked down sadly. Ann said "Um… Yeah, they picked up one of our pies before they left."

Sena didn't seem convinced at all. Sena said, "You are hiding something from me aren't you?" Thomas said "I am not supposed to tell you this but since you are their kid you deserve to know. Well, you are probably wondering why we are on this planet yet we don't seem to fit in with some of its other inhabitants right?" Sena said, "Yeah and?"

Ann said "Well we are not of this planet we are from a planet far away, a place with incredible technological advances. We were sent here as part of a colonization effort. Why? Because, currently our race is at war with other hybrid races and to ensure our species survives we had to find other planets to inhabit just in case of planetary extinction." Sena said, "So what does this mean for us, shouldn't my parents have been allowed to stay here?"

Thomas said, "In theory they should however now that you are more grown up, they were called back to do some dispatch. Our troops lead by Commander Kick Your Ass, Lieutenant Lightning, and General Gunships are fighting it out on the ground in space and even by air and sea. The battle is happening on Canis Major, Canis Minor, and our own Planet Neko. In the midst of it, all Canis Major Leader Wolfenstein Von Bark Bark is spearheading the full assault on our planet. Backed up only by Canis Minor Leader K-9. Your parents were sent to defend our planet and they are currently MIA. They could be dead or a prisoner to those sick bastards." Ann said, "I am sorry Sena but, at this time it doesn't look like your parents will return anytime soon." Sena broke down into tears and was hugged by Ann and Thomas.

Thomas said, "In short, we cannot give you the memories that were stolen from you Neko but, we can remind you of what we remember. Beyond that, we can only pray that whatever the wolves and dogs do, it doesn't jeopardize our chances of being equal among the humans globally, should we want or need a new planet to live on." Ann said, "It just occurred to me if wherever you were kept was a place you ran away from they might still have what you seek. But, don't go in there unprepared." Neko and Sena nodded.

Meanwhile, in Alcatraz Island Caleb returned from the Death Valley base having managed to quell the uprising of giant monsters. Caleb said, "Sir I have handled the threat in Death Valley my next mission?" Emperor Destroy Yu said, "Excellent, with that out of the way we can get back to work on other tasks." Caleb said, "Also while I was out there, I spotted something besides the mutants." Emperor Destroy Yu said "Eh? What would that be?" Caleb said, "It appeared to be a factory of sorts that said 'Neko Cola' on it." Emperor Destroy Yu said, "Why would I care about a soft drink production facility?" Caleb said, "Because, it smelled like dead bodies and was clearly not one of your listed bases at all."

Emperor Destroy Yu scratched his chin trying to make sense of all this. Emperor Destroy Yu said, "I'll let my men know to be on guard for anything suspicious. In the meantime, please return to the Manufactory. Caleb nodded and went into another room.

General Guillotine ran into Emperor Destroy Yu's office. General Guillotine said, "Sir, Neko could be on his way back here any moment he is after his memories. What should we do?" Emperor Destroy Yu said, "Damn it, I should have taken memories of his name and abilities too. Then he wouldn't be on his way back for the rest. It is clear we cannot afford to make any errors now. I didn't want it to come to this but, it seems we may only be able to have one since the other will not serve us. Send some Ninja out with our contract and our terms. We'll give him one last chance to serve us." General Guillotine did as commanded and about 10 Ninjas were sent out to handle this.

Back in Julian California Neko and Sena were sitting down to an excellent dinner of Roasted Turkey and Stuffing, Mashed Potatoes, and Cranberry Sauce. When the meal was finished, Ann brought out a Pumpkin Pie with whipped cream on it. Both Neko and Sena had a couple slices of it, as did Thomas and Ann. When they were full, Ann put away any leftovers and suddenly the sound of something sharp being thrown was heard. The family stood at attention. The object was thrown into the wall and happened to be a kunai.

A lone ninja walked in and introduced himself. The ninja said, "My name is Assn, the Assassin Ninja." Neko said, "Well Assn, what is the meaning of the kunai in our wall?" Assn said, "It was a warning throw. A 'General Guillotine' sent me for you." Neko said, "You mean that person who captured me and put me in a lab?" Assn said, "Yes precisely. And don't think of trying to retrace your way to the base you were in. Your enemies have cleverly switched to a base far away from here so you won't find them unless you agree to come work for us." Neko asked, "By us what is this organization you represent?" Assn said, "The B.D.S.M. Empire. Your brother knows us as the National Military Research & Development Association." Neko asked, "Why the variation in the name?"

Assn said, "Mainly to keep you and your brother on a different page in hopes that he would unknowingly make machines for a militant force outside the actual military."

Assn continued, "Since you were intelligent enough to figure out our intent when we captured you, there is no use hiding it anymore. By now you are well aware that you are on a planet where except small colonies like this one, your species is entirely unheard of. You know already you are an alien to this world. Think about it, if you join us, you could usher in a new world order where your species can coexist with humans. Better yet, you could have those who oppose us be your slaves for life. For too long people have been blinded by religion, spirituality, freedom and the like." Assn said, "Freedom is a lie even if we have the will to do what we want the way life is set up those who don't do what someone higher up than them says they don't get paid and they don't live on."

Assn asked, "How is that freedom? Huh?" Assn continued his rant, "And religion has made considerable unrest everywhere it exists since the dawn of time. Only through a dictatorship, can organic life forms hope to prosper. With all that in mind, all you need to do to make it happen is sign on the dotted line and work for us." Neko asked, "And if I refuse?" Assn said, "It is curtains for your parents, you have 5 minutes to discuss this amongst yourselves."

Neko turned to his parents unsure of himself. Thomas said, "Neko I know how you feel right now, you want more than anything for us to remain alive and to love you. I am sorry that when we sent you away, we were blind to the fact that you didn't feel loved because of what you were. Think about what you are doing. If you end up joining them and taking over humanity, how do you know they won't kill you once they've no use for you? Secondly, even if you did take over the world, would it be worth living in?"

Ann said "What your father said is true. Honestly, I would rather die, than live in a world where we have to do everything we are told or be put to death. I understand you wish for our species to be allowed to coexist here and not have to hide from Area 51 among others but, you won't accomplish it by working for them." Ann asked, "What if they fail?" Ann continued, "I know you are smarter and more resourceful than this entire army put together. Please just refuse even if they kill us!" Sena held him close and said, "Neko…"

Assn said, "Time's up did you make a decision?" Neko said, "Yes, I have decided no matter what you do I will not work for you." Assn said, "How brave but alas…"

He swiftly threw two Kunai at the throats of Neko's Mom and Dad causing blood to spurt out of their necks like a geyser as they bled to death in a matter of seconds. Neko fell to his knees and began crying silently in the midst of it. Sena held him comfortingly with tears in her eyes as well. Assn said "Well then now that you know we are serious, I'll give you one final chance. Sign or Sena is next." Neko said "Ok! I will do it!" He signed on the dotted line. Neko said, "Ok I signed now if I could, I would like an opportunity to build something for you right now. I want to show my gratitude for showing me the error of my ways."

Assn sighed and said, "Alright I may be an assassin but, I still remember my family so, I'll grant you this much." Neko said, "Thanks." Sena asked, "Neko what are you doing?" Neko winked at her slyly. Neko yelled, "Silence I am working here!" He grabbed some scrap metal that he'd collected a long time ago and began constructing a robot within mere minutes. Assn got up when Neko was finished. Neko said, "It is ready sir, would you like to do the honors of activating it?" Assn seeming slightly amused said, "Sure why not…" He pressed the on switch on the robot and it grabbed him by the throat. Assn said weakly, "Why you traitorous little shit!"

Neko smiled and asked ruefully, "Did you honestly think I'd just submit to your demands after what you did to my parents?" Neko said, "Fat chance of that!" Assn's neck was crushed and he could no longer breathe as he died a slow and painful death. His ninja minions ran back to HQ to report the news to Emperor Destroy Yu. Emperor Destroy Yu got the news and was outraged. Emperor Destroy Yu said, "Why that little shit he'll…" Suddenly Emperor Destroy Yu got a fiendish Idea. Emperor Destroy Yu dismissed the ninjas for now.

Caleb was called in. Caleb said, "Yes?" Emperor Destroy Yu said, "I have some rather grim news for you. Your parents just died." Caleb asked in disbelief, "What?! Who or what did it?" Emperor Destroy Yu said, "Your younger brother Neko." Caleb said, "But how why? What could have possessed him to do that?" Emperor Destroy Yu said, " I don't know but because you have been a good engineer and soldier to boot I have decided to give you a reward. For your hard work, we are mobilizing an army to help you get to the bottom of this and perhaps even take out the one so despicable as to kill their own parents in cold blood."

Caleb said, "No offense sir but leave your 'soldiers' out of this he is mine! I will handle him myself. I will however, need tons of machines to bring with me as he is probably building his own army about now if he is as good at what he does like me." Emperor Destroy Yu said, "As you wish chief mechanic!"

Meanwhile back in Julian Neko was in Sena's Arms Mourning the parents. Sena said, "Neko I understand how you feel right now but, I have a feeling we haven't seen the last of them. More may yet be on their way and we need to prepare for war." Neko nodded and said, "You are right, as much as it hurts to lose loved ones, I cannot let my emotions get us both killed." Neko ran off to a local Junkyard. Sena followed him. Neko said, "Alright we don't know what kinds of troops we'll be facing so we'll want to have mechanical forces to handle anything." Sena nodded. Neko and Caleb began crafting Infantry a Tank and Some Airstrike robots as well as some that attack from underground. They both made some Scorpion Tanks, which are tanks that looked like scorpions but, had missile launchers on their backs and had a machine gun and laser gun attachment. The lasers are powerful enough to vaporize organic and inorganic life forms with some exceptions. After finishing the advanced weapons, they took a rest for the night.

9 INVASION TIME
Battle of the Brothers!

When dawn came, Neko awoke to a rumbling sound on the ground. Sena was shaking him awake, "Neko wake up they are attacking!" Neko said, "Sena, get in the tank, it will protect you from enemy fire." She nodded and did as commanded. Neko commanded a wave of Infantry to attack the opposing infantry. Panicked civilians packed their bags and tried desperately to evacuate the place. There was no way to escape the massive amounts of militant forces on their way so, the civilians hid in their homes. The B.D.S.M. Empire was following close behind Caleb's portion of the army as a backup unit. Both Caleb's army and the rest of the B.D.S.M. Empire came by air flying over the Pacific Ocean towards Carlsbad where they came in for a landing just outside Julian California. This massive wave of enemy units didn't go unnoticed by the military and police of the surrounding areas.

The National Guard came in to rescue the civilians hiding in their homes to minimize casualties from the uprising. The civilians except for Neko and Sena were evacuated. Any hybrids that were picked up, were taken to Area 51 for interrogation and other things done at that base. Emperor Destroy Yu was back at his Death Valley base with Lieutenant Laser. Emperor Destroy Yu said, "Damn it General Guillotine and Caleb have been found if we don't think quickly our quest for world domination is as good as failed." Lieutenant Laser said, "Sir I believe that we have worse problems at the moment." Emperor Destroy Yu said, "And what is that?" Lieutenant Laser said, "That factory Caleb found some hybrids were being taken into it as prisoners." Emperor Destroy Yu said, "And that hurts us how?" Lieutenant Laser said, "Our scouts snuck into it briefly and some wolf and dog hybrids appear to be operating it. Some cat hybrids were in cages." Emperor Destroy Yu said, "Oh shit! How will we ever take over the world if the only hope for doing so lies in factions at war?"

Lieutenant Laser said, "Exactly with that and the recklessness of Caleb and General Guillotine, I believe we are at a standstill as far as finding a means of world domination."

39

Emperor Destroy Yu said, "I'll rule this world yet, mark thine words. It may not be today or tomorrow but someday when the time is right, I'll claim this world as my own." Emperor Destroy Yu went to the Manufactory and Copied Caleb's schematic and engineering techniques with some help some of the machines Caleb made as army units preparing to attack anyone or anything that comes their way.

Meanwhile back in Julien again; Neko, Caleb, and General Guillotine were fighting off military units as well as each other. Caleb, General Guillotine, and Neko were not within sight of one another. They only saw military units from, the United States; Army, Navy, National Guard, Marines, and a slew of robots of all kinds fighting back and forth.

Neko said, "Sena this is getting high profile and ruinous. We need to get out of here quickly!" Sena said, "Yeah at this rate this place will be in ruins." Neko said, "Good thing I have my trump card. Bazooka!" He shot military aircraft out of the sky while his makeshift planes rained down fire on ground units while minimizing property damage. Caleb did exactly the same forcing the military to retreat for now the ones that remained. Caleb finally showed himself after both he and Neko had taken out about an equal amount of each other's units. Neko asked, "Caleb what do you think you are doing?" Caleb said, "I could ask you the same, murderer!" Neko said, "What? Until today, I didn't kill anyone!" Caleb said, "Bullshit! Emperor Destroy Yu, head of the National Military Research & Development Association said that you killed our parents." Caleb asked, "Why did you do it?" Neko said, "I didn't do it!"

Neko asked, "Don't you find it a bit suspicious, they asked you out of the blue to join a secret military research group when you aren't even on the grid or documented in this country?" Neko continued, "Second of all 'Emperor Destroy Yu' took my memories in hopes I would work for him without you or I knowing we both worked for him." Neko said, "According to one of his agents he plans to take over the world. Judging from the fact he told you I did this when I have no motive to kill our parents, it would seem we've been duped into killing each other!"

Suddenly General Guillotine showed up clapping villainously. He said, "Congratulations Neko, you figured out our plan!

Emperor Destroy Yu is making machines off your brother's schematics as we speak. As such we have no further use for you Caleb but thanks so much for your help so far." He jumped up and Shot Caleb Point blank in the head repeatedly. Caleb's Spirit slowly ascended to the heavens and said, "Remember Neko we were trained to make exactly the same things so, you know the weakness of these things. I am sorry, I didn't see through their plan sooner. Goodbye and good luck." Neko got really pissed off and Jumped into his tank. General Guillotine got into the military tank Caleb Made.

Neko said, "Sena you drive I'll shoot! Kite maneuver now!" Sena said, "Roger that!" By this point, the units Caleb and Neko had made to this point had canceled each other out and it was just Neko and General Guillotine. Neko's tank encircled General Guillotines driven by Sena and shot it 20 times, before it broke down and launched General Guillotine out of it. Once out of the Tank General Guillotine kneeled in front of Neko's Tank. General Guillotine said, "Please Neko I beg of you, I can change just don't kill me. I will do anything have mercy!" Neko asked, "'Mercy?' After what your people did to my Mom and Dad and what you did to my brother Caleb?" Neko said, "You are barking up the wrong tree pal!" Neko took one last shot with his tank's cannon and in a flash of a tank cannon blast, General Guillotine was naught but a smoldering pile of ash.

Neko said, "Sena excellent driving, I need to get out of here and so do you. If you stay here who knows what might happen. If you run away with me, things may not be much better. So what will you do?" Sena said, "I will come with you. As long as Area 51 remains a threat to our people, we aren't safe in this place. We are now on the grid as a place that hid aliens." Neko said, "Good point, let's go!" Neko pulled up a digital map in the tank. Neko said "If we go northwest we will run into Covina, Temecula, and Los Angeles from there. If we go west, we will hit Carlsbad and Escondido and possibly Tijuana. If we go east from here, we hit the Salton Sea, the Colorado River Reservation, and eventually Phoenix Arizona. If we go a bit more north after Traveling east, we should hit Las Vegas. Hmm, we could try going for San Bernardino County that seems to be the next closest county that might let us live there. Then again we'd be best to hide somewhere with Desert Mirages. Death Valley seems like it would fit the bill, or maybe one of the lakes in Nevada like Walker Lake or Lake Mead."

Sena said, "Please Neko, for the love of g-d choose somewhere now!" Neko said, "Fine, Death Valley should suffice. It will be hot enough that most enemies won't live a long time on foot and it is remote enough not to be an obvious place to look for us. Furthermore it isn't an impossible path to travel." Sena said, "Good thinking now let's go!" Neko said, "We'll never get there in this tank." Neko got out and quickly used broken scrap parts to construct a private jet plane and the rest were made into robots like the scorpion robots and mechanized infantry he'd been using up till now. He crafted some solar panels so it could run on solar energy for now instead of gasoline. Neko said, "Someday I'll learn how to harness desert heat and the very essence of outer space and nature to fuel my inventions but, for now, this should suffice."

10 THE NEKO HOTEL AND RESORT
The Hideout!

Sena and Neko got into the private Jet Plane and they flew for about an hour or less to reach Bad Water Basin. Sena looked outside and said "Yuck! Now I know why they call it Bad Water Basin!" Neko said, "Nothing a little cleaning couldn't fix." Neko reprogrammed about 8 robots that were once infantry for cleaning and building and 4 more for service, the rest remained defense units. Soon the robots were hard at work cleaning and purifying the bad water into drinkable natural tasting water that could be used for staying hydrated among other things.

Neko said, "You know with it being hot as it is here, this oasis in the desert can be a lovely day spa." Sena said, "Yeah you are right and with enough building materials perhaps we can establish a hotel and resort." After about 6 hours of construction, Neko's robots built a lovely air conditioned day spa storefront. It wasn't more than a couple hours, before some tourists came by. They had braved the heat and were lost in the desert. To make a long story short, these people were pampered and well taken care of. Neko made some agricultural robots to plant some seeds of fruit indigenous to desert highlands and a few tropical fruit trees among others. His mining robots that he crafted and programmed over the next few weeks, began gathering supplies to upgrade the robots and even some items to be used to build a base.

After About four months of intensive agricultural work, mining, hospitality services, and construction, a hotel and resort about ten stories high had been built. To those in the desert or in the sky, it could easily be dismissed as a mirage and was painted to blend in well with the sand and other natural things surrounding it for that purpose. Neko said, "Well, after all, this time, we finally have our hideout. My clock says it is December 15, 2000, C.E.

Neko said, "I am really glad the residents here have agreed not to tell anyone where we are not that anyone would believe them." Sena said, "Yeah and someday we'll find a way to leave this planet and return to our home one." Neko said, "Yeah but until then this is our little piece of land where we can do anything we want. You just can't put a price on that kind of freedom." By this point and time, the residents of Julien moved back in, and their properties repaired.

Neko said, "I can't help thinking, I've forgotten something, though." Sena said, "Um Neko I am Pregnant again…" Neko asked, "Wait what again, what do you mean again?" Sena said, "Yeah when we had our first time, when I was 4 years old. I got pregnant with a lovely baby boy who looked like you but my parents took him with her when they left on their important business. He could still be out there somewhere." Neko said, "Then I have to know that he is safe. I have to find a way off this planet. Time is of the essence."

Meanwhile at the Neko Cola Factory. Wolfenstein Von Bark Bark was getting updates from his own scouts and factory workers. Canis asked, "What, There are a hotel and resort and a rogue human organization out here?" Scout Lookout said, " Yes, but that isn't all it would seem that in the southern portion of Nevada in the western United States, 83 miles (134 km) north-northwest of Las Vegas. Situated at its center, on the south shore of Groom Lake, is a large military airfield. Some hybrids of not just Nekos but other dog and wolf species were taken in by these 'humans.' Some of our scouts were captured and taken there.

Wolfenstein Von Bark Bark asked, "But how? We have much better military technology than them. We should have had no problem taking them out!" Scout Lookout said "It isn't that simple. You see when one of the Nekos brought in their tech to battle the tech of another, they nearly destroyed an entire town in a matter of minutes while trying to outdo one another. The ones they captured were civilians who we sent to colonize this place in case of planetary extinction. As for the scouts they were outnumbered and taken by surprise. You didn't exactly fit them with anti-spy gear or military grade weaponry."

Wolfenstein Von Bark Bark growled, "These humans want war they got war!" Back at The Neko Hotel & Resort, Sena was urging Neko to call off the search for his son to handle more domestic issues. Sena said, "Neko please before you go after your son did you not see our people get taken away by the human race during your battle? I transported back to Julian California and all the hybrids were gone, even though the humans returned there. I asked the humans and they said the hybrids were most likely taken to Area 51." Neko said, "Alright our first mission is to rescue our friends. To the Nekocoptor!" A cheesy superhero transition covered the screen if this was an animated story of some sort or visual novel.

Neko said, "Hold down the Fort Sena, I'll be back!" Sena nodded and Neko left in a helicopter that looked like him. He put it in stealth mode so, the human technology wouldn't detect him as he got nearer to the base. Wolfenstein Von Bark Bark got into a Stealth Plane and K9 got into a Stealth Zeppelin and Emperor Destroy Yu ordered Lieutenant Laser to take a Stealth Digger, which was a digging drill vehicle shaped like a mole.

11 ESCAPE FROM AREA 51
A Traitor Among them!

Meanwhile, in Area 51 Interrogator Ian came to the cages of the captured Cat people Dog people and Wolf People and yes even Fox people. Ian asked, "Do any of you speak English?" They all said, "Yes." Ian said, "Good, now tell us how long you have been hiding among us." A lone Neko with Blond hair and Blue eyes that anyone could mistake as a clone of Neko himself stepped forward. He said, "First off you can call me Nekki Qui, secondly, we have been on earth since the Middle Ages at least. We have disguised ourselves to hide from you but, you cannot contain us forever. Sooner or later someone will find out about what you are doing here, and they will come for us. We never meant anyone any harm, you see just as your race has had its share of wars so have ours. The original plan was to study your ways and learn from your mistakes but, then unrest broke out among our races. We needed a place to call home in case of planetary extinction."

Ian said, "Hmm fascinating indeed, you seem pretty earnest albeit a bit overconfident." Nekki Qui said, "We don't care if humans rule this place or not, we just want a place for those who want nothing to do with the war to live. However, if your people cannot even grant us this, we will do what is necessary to achieve our goal and make a refuge for ourselves here." Ian left the room to ponder what had just happened. At this point another human within the Facility came into the room. Her name was Deloris Double Agent.

Deloris Double Agent said, "Nekki Qui was it?" Nekki Qui said "Yes?" Deloris said, "I am Deloris Double Agent and it is my belief, that what our people are doing here is wrong. Interrogating life forms that just want the freedoms we claim to represent and cherish, dissecting them like they were frogs in a science class. It is disgusting! Worse still, they've been experimenting to create weird mythical beasts from Greek mythology."

Deloris continued, "This is supposed to be a place of secret weapons so we have the upper hand in case Russia or other terrorist supporting countries, think they can just come in here and threaten our great nation! I'll let you out, now go and do what you have to do!"

She opened the cages and the alarms rang. She then went as far as letting out the mutant experiments, to keep the other agents busy while the hybrids and furries escaped. Deloris ran out of the building and teleported away.

Nekki Qui said, "Wow she sure is brave. Nekki Qui pulled out a compact Defibrillator Gun in the case of mechanical guards and a small Vaporizer in the other hand for organic life forms. The Vaporizer is known for turning organic life forms into dust literally, while the defibrillator shuts down mechanical units. He and the other hybrids and furries used similar weapons to his and shot their way out of the base just as Neko got there and so did Wolfenstein Von Bark Bark and Lieutenant Laser.

The guards in their towers were about to fire on the escapees when some experimental Minotaur leaped up and knocked the men out of their towers. Some soldiers from a weapons testing facility not more than 300 yards away came in as, Neko was evacuating hybrids. Neko said, "Damn it they won't all fit in this helicopter, I need something bigger." Sena flew in with reinforcements in a series of airplanes big enough to fit a couple thousand people per plane. Neko said, "Excellent work Sena!" Everybody into the planes!" The escaped hybrids all filled the airplanes Lieutenant Laser used some of the BDSM Empire's Machines to distract and hold off the opposing soldiers. Neko saw this and was shocked even Wolfenstein Von Bark Bark was fighting alongside him and K 9.

Neko asked, "What is the meaning of this?" Lieutenant Laser said, "Our organization's primary objective is world domination. We cannot do it without the hybrids. Emperor Destroy Yu never said exactly 'how,' to take over the world just 'to,' take over the world." Wolfenstein Von Bark Bark said, "Our species may not be friends with the cat people but, these guys are apparently bent on controlling anything that isn't human. I'll be damned if these 'Humans' rule the universe! Besides, they took my Son Ruff Ruff!" K9 said, "They took K10 my successor, I cannot rest until I know that he is in a position to rule my planet." Neko said, "Alright I'll be taking the hybrids, they'll be safe in my secret base." Neko and Sena Flew off leaving the three of them to hold off the remaining forces. Once they were gone, the three helpful entities were teleported back to their base. This left any remaining fighters wondering wtf just happened. Lieutenant Laser asked, "Boss? Did you do that?"

Emperor Destroy Yu said, "Yes, Caleb left a schematic to an emergency Teleporter. Good work out there. With the hybrids free and the Area 51 agents thrown off, maybe now we can plan our next move to dominate the world." Lieutenant Laser asked, "Still on the world domination thing?" Lieutenant Laser said, "Face it you got technology from one person and we've managed to survive so far, but I feel your plans are too ambitious." Emperor Destroy Yu said, "Caleb wouldn't have helped us if he knew we were out to rule the world so, I had to drop him. General Guillotine was a tragic loss, but he wasn't anything special. But, you are a cut above him you knew when to fight alongside the enemy. When to lull them into a false sense of security and when to attack them."

Emperor Destroy Yu said, "For now, we'll let the hybrids have their war if this is their goal and while they are fighting we'll steal their technology and send it to each Nation's Capital. Then we'll rule it all. Not even Area 51 has the means to stop an assault like that."

Meanwhile, the hybrids were getting settled in at The Neko Hotel & Resort. K10 said, "Wow nice base you have here, Neko. Ruff Ruff said, "Eh it is a little primitive compared to what I am used to technologically but, at least the air and water are fresh here. I suppose one won't do much better in the middle of nowhere." Nekki Qui said, "I'd say this is pretty standard, our people aren't big on technology that leaves a huge carbon footprint. Even though our Sun is artificial. We like technology that improves the lives of others and is highly efficient, despite not being that impressive or seemingly uninspired."

Neko said, "Hey… Nekki Qui was it?" Nekki Qui said, "What is it, father?" Neko said, "What?" Nekki Qui said, "I am the son you had with Sena when you were four years old." Neko teared up happily and said, "Oh wow, I have been looking for you!" Neko gave Nekki Qui a huge hug and licked his cat ears like a loving father. Nekki Qui said, "Father! Stop it! You are embarrassing me in front of the future rulers of our warring factions." Suddenly a heavy knock at the door was heard. Neko answered it to find K9 and Wolfenstein Von Bark Bark outside. Neko asked, "What is it now?" Wolfenstein Von Bark Bark said, "I believe these two belong to you." They threw Sena's Parents at her. Sena yelled, "Mommy Daddy I missed you so much!" She hugged them both tightly. K 9 asked, "Now can we have our sons back?"

Neko said, "Sure take them." K 10 and Ruff Ruff ran to their father. The four of them left for their home planet.

12 UNHOLY ALLIANCES
The Forsakenists & The new Las Vegas Mafia

Emperor Destroy Yu put on a trench coat and took a suspicious vehicle to the city of Las Vegas, Nevada. He arranged to meet with a shadowy figure, who might have some ties with a reemergence of a mafia. In a back alley in the dead of night, he went to the location in question. The anonymous person whispered, "Hey the name is Louie our 'associates' are waiting for you." The Emperor nodded and attended the meeting that was held inside. Louie said "Alright boys our associate is here. I believe our boss, would like to explain the situation."

The mafia boss nodded and said, "Emperor Destroy Yu, I am Don Giovanni of the New Las Vegas Mafia. Ever since the 1990s, loyalty has been a bit hard to find. Mafia groups are turning each other in for protection and sustenance for life by the government. My grandparents remember a time before all that, when life was good and no one fucked with us. Well, except our wives or anyone we wanted to score with but, that is beside the point." Emperor Destroy Yu said, "That sounds all well and nice, but you know what I am here for right?" Don Giovanni replied, "Yes, as I understand it you and your outstanding scientists and engineers need a new hideout. You also need to conduct business and take care of a few meddlesome pests eh?"

Emperor Destroy Yu said, "Exactly and I am willing to make a few robots, that you can use to reclaim Las Vegas for your own. No longer must you lose important men to police now you have a militia to help you. Claim this place and let me operate here as I see fit to attack a particular cat person and this city is otherwise yours to control as are the machines I grant you."

Don Giovanni said, "We have ourselves a deal. However, my informants tell me that a bit west of here in San Dimas there is a resistance force building. Apparently some people 'disappeared' real mysteriously like. While some youths who heard the reports have bravely dared each other to visit Covina." Emperor Destroy Yu asked, "And I should care why?" Don Giovanni said "Because, it is unclear what the motives of any of those forces are. We don't know whether they intend to head east towards us or proceed further west and north. I wouldn't go there if I were you."

Emperor Destroy Yu nodded and walked outside to be escorted to his new hideout and he began building machines for this new organization based on the ones he'd made before.

Meanwhile, in Covina Adam, The Forsaken was in his hideout with Christina. Adam said, "Good work trading with the humans again, Christina they have no idea that one of their own is working against them." Christina smiled and said, "But of course, Adam we have these beautiful kitty children now and we cannot live in a world that will not accept your kind." Christina said, "Also Adam since you don't seek to necessarily rule this world but, just want a place to be you, I had an idea you might like." Adam raised an eyebrow amused and said, "Go on." Christina said, "Well, even though the humans don't know it was you who destroyed Covina and they would have no way to prove it, there are some people building organizations to take back Covina and West Covina. They are getting support from their government. You are now one of the most wanted people ever to fly under the radar." Adam smirked his eyes turned red under the influence of the spirits within him. Adam said, "So what was your idea? I am 'dying' to know."

Christina said, "Alright Adam well I saw some children and teenagers making plans to sneak out of surrounding cities. They want to come and check this place out before the armies come in. These children are outcasts, geeks, dweebs, goths, emo kids, and basically anyone who isn't popular. As it turns out, some are human and some have been pretending to be human for a while." Adam said, "And I should care why?" Christina said, "Well you may be able to control the dead but, isn't it nice to have a fan club or perhaps a few cultists you can count on for things the dead can't? Or if naught else a little extra support?" Adam said "Alright go ahead and let them in but you know what will happen to them if this is a trick. I need to go to my Necromancer room so I can perform a ritual to further attune myself."

Christina nodded and began accepting the new recruits while, Adam meditated. Adam looked within himself and saw the spirit of the book of necromancy. The spirit said, "I have been waiting for you, Adam." Adam said, "Who are you?" The spirit showed itself to be what looked to be a plague doctor with the beaked mask.

It said, "I am Astriedax Hallejah from Medieval England. I was one of King Henry III finest plague doctors and for years, I studied things under his nose that were at the time forbidden. When the bubonic plague hit England, I was finally given more leash to study my arcane arts in hopes of having a back door solution to it. While trying to discover a cure for it, I instead found a secret to immortality. However it wasn't the kind of immortality that most people would desire." Adam said, "So I am going to take a wild guess and say that instead of finding the cure or immortality, you figured out a way to bring back the dead." Astriedax Hallejah said, "You are correct. However, I was caught when I'd summoned a low-level zombie by King Henry III. His guards promptly killed it and I was sentenced to be hung from the gallows."

Adam said, "Then why have you chosen me to wield your powers?" Astriedax Hallejah said, "Because, you like me know what it is to be misunderstood to have the best intent in the world and be punished for being yourself."

Astriedax Hallejah continued, "But, be warned young cat boy should your anger or sadness get out of control or fear, the powers will control you like they did when you attacked the people who had wronged you." Adam said, "So it wasn't you that attacked the ones I hated?" Astriedax Hallejah said, "No I am just the medium through which the powers are channeled. The first necromancer." Adam said, "If you are from England why was the book written in Hebrew?" Astriedax Hallejah said, "I needed a way to disguise my studies, I put it in a language I thought King Henry III didn't know. I may have underestimated him, though. I thought that since his the Jews were forced out of England in 1290 by his Grandfather King Henry I, that none of the royal family would know Hebrew. So that book you wield is the culmination of my research and words you can use to control the restless undead. It was all I could do before being put to death."

Astriedax Hallejah continued, "Also, be warned the ones that were slain will come back to get you sooner or later. You can keep them under control by either killing people or carving words into your arm or having someone else cut you up somehow." Adam said, "How often should I have to do this?" Astriedax Hallejah said, "Well considering you slew so many you have complete control over the ones in my book, but those that aren't yet attuned to the book will need a blood sacrifice before you can capture them." Adam said, "There is just one thing." Astriedax Hallejah asked, "Yes?" Adam asked, "How did you become one with the book like this?"

Astriedax Hallejah said, "Upon being put to death, my soul was swallowed by the book and now I am the personification of everything evil within it. For centuries, I've had some different holders. None of whom were worthy of harnessing the powers of this book, and then you came along." Adam said, "So basically from England to the new land other mysterious entities like me picked up the book and carried it here until eventually it was rediscovered and donated to a library?" Astriedax Hallejah said, "That is the simplest answer for it however, you may be aware that those unworthy got sucked into it when they tried to take it from you right?" Adam replied, "Yes."

Astriedax Hallejah said, "That only happens when the chosen necromancer has opened it. The reason it didn't happen before is because the one destined to awaken it hadn't yet opened it. Without that happening it would have only been a strange book in Hebrew letters to anyone else. So no one had any reason to think the magic inside it existed. The one who ultimately brought it to the library was a Wiccan. She thought it might contain a new form of magic but, couldn't read it. She happened to be in Covina and dropped it off at the Library."

Adam said, "That makes a lot more sense. I am sensing entities with strange energy signatures now." Astriedax said, "That is part of the attunement ritual. You can now sense other entities like yourself." Adam said, "There are two in Yosemite National Park, another in Torrance, one in Death Valley, Nevada. I also sense several forces preparing an attack, this could be big." Astriedax nodded and said, "Yes, you must prepare to take them on. It won't be longer than a year before they make their move. Ready yourself, this could very well be a battle for the world itself and we cannot be concerned with the other entities outside our reach. We have to protect what is ours. We can worry about them once all of our known domestic issues are solved. So; make this a refuge for all who have even a tuft of fur on their chests, heads, or tails and welcome all who will fight for you in." Adam finally came out of the meditation as Christina was bringing in the "Forsakenists."

Adam began the meeting of the Forsakenists with Christina bringing snacks and drinks. The meeting was held in the "Covina Play House." Adam asked, "Alright humans, hybrids, furries, and whatever. I understand you all are aware that people who came here had a tendency to 'disappear' correct?" They nodded. Adam continued, "Well I found a book of amazing abilities and long story short the powers were too much for me to handle. As a result this place is a ghost town in both senses of the word."

A dead silence filled the room. Adam said, "I know I know, listen I don't want to rule the world or anything a cliché cartoon or other media may portray those of the dark side to want. All I wanted was to live life on my own terms, not get my ass kicked by every last human who saw me, and to be the righteous cat person I was brought up to be. My parents, when they saw what I could do, ran away. I couldn't bring myself to kill them. I knew that although, they weren't around when stuff was getting horrible for me, they tried to help. But, there was nothing they could do. They made the right choice leaving me here alone. You guys or girls or whatever you identify as, I know you are different than the rest. You too know what it is to be treated like trash by others, to be sneered at, to be alone inside, and to be in the wrong time period or place. I know how it feels more than you know, I was there. So, I grant you this opportunity of a lifetime. You can have a haven worth living in on earth. One that allows you to live life on your own terms and find what it is you do best and do it. Or you can go back to your families, forget you ever saw me and hope that your families won't be in the wrong place at the worst time. Many different factions will vie for control of this site and others like it. War is coming and you must choose wisely. Live here and I shall protect you all with my life, leave and I hope you have adequate life insurance or protection wherever you are. Make your choice."

They spoke it over for a while before having someone speak for them. It was a young African American female human. She said, "The name is Danielle and I believe I speak for us all when I say we can all relate to your plight. Though it is questionable if death was the answer, no matter what we do from here on out there is a risk that we will die. So, if that is to be our fate, we shall do so fighting for what we believe in!"

Adam said, "Very well then, I shall grant each of you a few helpful abilities." He flipped through his Book of Necromancy and found a spell that enabled him to give dark powers to others. He cast the spell and all in the room could now shoot dark flames out of their hands and feet. They could use it to fly like a rocket or blast enemies away or roast their enemies. They could also summon a few dark creatures as well and cast dark versions of all kinds of elements. This includes dark ice, dark earth, and dark lightning. Basically, any form of a magic could be turned dark and used in addition to the dark flames.

Furthermore, if they had physical abilities such as martial arts, those were heightened significantly. All were in awe of their new powers and grateful.

Adam said, "Remember these dark forces are not just weapons of war but, also your shields too. Remember well the darkness and you may portal out of dangerous situations and raise a shield to protect yourselves. Remember well who it was who allowed you to manifest your destiny and never forget why you sought to be endarkened." The Forsakenists, were about to leave the meeting and claim their new homes and businesses, when Adam interrupted them. Adam said, "Before you go, remember 'Mom's Not Here!' If you hear that someone's time is up." They nodded and left the base preparing for the inevitable war.

With that, we turn our attention away from Adam and friends and back to the real character of this story. Not to worry there will be more of this to come in the second series and possibly in book 3.

Adam said, "Hey writer, that isn't fair you got these readers all excited and for what?" The author responded with a tired sigh, "All things in good time my friend." Adam asked, "The 'real character of this story?' Without me, no one could relate to any of this at all. Also, people typically pay their actors you know." The writer responded, "I would but, how am I going to get the money in my world into yours?" Adam said, "Write the payment into the story. It won't cost you anything!" The writer replied, "No, sorry you have to earn it through events in the story as everyone else. Besides you have more than enough toys and things in that abandoned mall in West Covina and all the small mom and pop shops you forced out of town." Adam said, "Now you make me sound like a Corporation." Both the Writer and Adam The Forsaken laughed, as the next chapter began on schedule.

13 PLANET NEKO
Home Bittersweet Home!

After a heartfelt reunion, Neko began asking Nekki Qui about his home planet. Neko asked, "Nekki? How do I reach Planet Neko?" Nekki Qui said, "It is in a whole other system outside the solar system. You would need a rocket capable of traveling at light speed or faster to reach it anytime soon." Neko asked, "Do you have a schematic for such a thing?" Nekki Qui said, "No I don't, they couldn't entrust me with such a thing. However, I will have to return soon. They need me to report back what happened here." Neko said, "Forget it, I'll figure out how to get there myself. I will have to apply everything I learned at The Furlington Academy." Nekki Qui said, "By the way Dad, I built you an emergency teleporter since you have now become part of the war. You should have one in case you need a quick escape. I even left you schematic in a safe place should it ever break." Neko said, "Thanks, son."

Neko and his construction bots were able to build a spaceship that could travel fast enough to reach Planet Neko in 6 Earth Hours. Neko breathed heavily after the hard work. Neko said, "Alright, Robots add a space ship feature like this one to our hotel and resort. I get the feeling I'll need it one day." The robots did as commanded. Neko said, "In the meantime, I have to call off this war. These dog and wolf hybrids are parents just like me and care about their offspring. Why must there be war with that being the case? Moreover, these 'humans' are significantly more xenophobic than anything I've ever encountered as a whole."

Neko got into his space ship and set the coordinates for Planet Neko using a galactic map that Nekki Qui happened to have on him. The coordinates were logged for future quick access use. His spaceship looked just like his head. Six hours of boring space travel later he landed on Planet Neko.

A crowd gathered around the spacecraft composing of a mix of armed soldiers in Hazmat suits and still others in typical commando gear. The civilians, however, were completely nude or at most in undergarments and sandals. This is to prevent their privates and feet from getting stuck to surfaces or cut. They also had belts that held laser swords and laser handguns at their waists.

Still others looked like they were on steroids apparently not needing weapons to do their fighting. Neko Said "Um I am sorry for my sudden landing here I came to speak with whoever is in charge here. A Commander showed up wearing the latest weapons and armor the planet had to offer. He said, "The name is Commander Kick Your Ass. This planet has no official leader all. It has a military composed of civilians and a few leader types like myself but we don't have what earthlings call a President, Emperor or King."

Commander Kick Your Ass continued, "There are a few tribe leaders and the like but no official form of government here that impacts everything." Neko said, "Well with all due respect sir, I am completely opposed to this war we are having with these dog things." Commander Kick Your Ass laughed condescendingly and said, "Foolish cat hybrid, you know nothing of what they've done to our people! Why even on that planet you called Earth, they have factories set up! Are you really so naïve to think we made our own soda brand to sell on earth, when there are far more important things to worry about?" Neko said, "No I don't, I didn't know there was such a factory."

Commander Kick Your Ass said, "Well listen here 'genius boy', those factories are conveniently disguised prison facilities for our people. They abducted our people and brought them there as collateral." Neko said, "Hold it back it up a bit, how did this war even begin?" Commander Kick Your Ass said, "Lead Historian Eureka come here please." Eureka asked, "Yes sir?" Kick Your Ass said, "This cat boy identified as Neko, wants to know about the War of the Dogs Wolves and Cats."

Eureka said, "Alright a long time ago about the medieval period on earth. We were beginning our galactic program to explore nearby planets Lead by GSA or Galactic Space Administration's Lead Scientist Professor Tick Tock Clockwork Bot." Neko said, "Um not to break the fourth wall here but is it just me or does almost everyone in this novel have a funny name?" Eureka got a phone call and said, "Historian Eureka speaking! Yes? Oh, I'll tell them." She hung up and said, "That was the fourth wall construction company, they told me to stop breaking their walls." Neko said, "Alright I will stop but, please go on I need to know more."

Eureka cleared her throat and resumed speaking, "Well then as I was saying Professor Tick Tock Clockwork Bot, and stop laughing at his name, sent out a team of researchers to find all the hybrid planets they could. Long story short after a few years they did but no one could have predicted the impact such intergalactic endeavors and enterprises could have had on the life forms. Once we'd found these planets and landed on them, their inhabitants studied the tech we brought and then a competition to make a better means of space travel began. It sounds all well and good to want to progress so quickly however, with advancement comes with it a set of consequences all its own. Thanks to the artificial suns the furry races made, the planets were quickly able to make in the wake of the Big Bang several species survived. Some chose to continue advancing further while others preferred to keep things mostly eco-friendly or natural. Others wanted a little of everything. We were in the last school, we wanted things to be a bit of everything."

Eureka continued, "That is there is one side of the planet dedicated to high-tech goodies while, the vast majority wanted to preserve the natural beauty of this place. If they accepted any advancements, the tech had to be eco-friendly. Fortunately, we were able to reach a compromise. Not every planet was as fortunate in that way." Eureka adjusted her glasses as she asked, "Now how could something so trivial turn into a war you must be thinking?" Eureka continued, "Well just as cats and dogs tend to be mortal enemies, as a sort of predator and prey relationship. The unique atmospheric conditions that made us, who would have otherwise been humans like the earthlings into hybrids and some even furries." Neko asked, "What are furries?"

Eureka said, "Furries are anthropomorphic beings that are almost entirely animal save their ability to walk upright and to speak as humans do. Hybrids are what we know as people who seem almost human enough but, can hide their features if needed. There are also hybrids that are of two different anthropomorphic animal species as well so, it gets confusing." Eureka explained, "Because, Hybrid species means 'two or more species in one', it is acceptable to call things that appear or are a cross between humans and furries hybrids."

Eureka continued her story, "So while we aren't necessarily half human half animal, we are essentially alien mutants in this case. Basically, with these animal instincts making it difficult for us to coexist with one another, all it took was a few seemingly trivial fights among our species before the dogs and wolves of Canis Major and Canis Minor had enough."

Eureka said, "Only in recent years have we seen an evolution to the point where our species has had any sort of control over our primal urges. Trouble is even with this now being possible old prejudices die hard. It's like the war on the Middle East on planet Earth."

Neko asked, "How is it like the war in the Middle East on planet Earth?" Eureka said, "Simple, even if the people fighting in it did so for anything sacred in it that isn't their only driving force. The driving force they all deny is keeping it going is their concept of 'An Eye for an Eye.' This policy continues to influence everything from politics to justice systems on the planet."

Neko said, "So the reason any war rages on at all is because, there are still citizens on all sides that wants to avenge the deaths of their loved ones over stuff they believe would otherwise be trivial now?" Eureka said, "To put it in the most immature light possible, yes." Neko said "Honestly I can relate, I showed no mercy at all to the humans who killed my loved ones. It has taken all my restraint not to lose myself and conquer it all." Eureka said, "Then you understand now, why this vicious cycle continues and why Commander Kick Your Ass is naturally cynical about it ever coming to an end."

Neko said, "Be that as it may I do believe we may have one thing that unites us all." Eureka said, "And that is?" Neko said, "Well with these primitive humans being at least as xenophobic about each other as well as ourselves, I think if we could focus the hate we had for each other on those who fear us, perhaps peace can yet be achieved." Commander Kick Your Ass said, "That is probably the smartest thing I've heard all year." Eureka said, "Have you any other questions?"

Neko said, "Well I don't know if this is that important but, I noticed despite the war there are so many of us some even look like me. What's more is they are out in the open and some are naked." Eureka said, "Well it is our season for mating and some cat people are nudists; because clothes are for earthlings unless they protect against radioactive materials, weather, or are needed as a disguise. The ritual goes that the asker cat person will initiate a tail wrap with another Cat person when in heat. This can happen either under the influence of catnip or cold weather. The consenter cat person will then, lick and suck on the asker's ears to say "yes." If the consenter doesn't want to procreate with someone, he or she will try and break the tail wrap by walking away and shaking his or her head."

Eureka continued, "It is rare that this ever happens, especially these days when we need to maintain our population. Secondly, we don't have double standards so, a female isn't a slut for wanting the same sex as a guy, nor is the guy a hero for doing so here. It is nothing more than a necessary thing to continue our population. The consent ritual I described is considered sacred, and sex should never be had without performing it!" Eureka said, "Fortunately, it is a natural instinct so, as long as a cat person doesn't breed with a human or species without a tail, they will do so without even thinking about it."

Neko asked, "And if they did with a human?" Eureka said, "They would probably stick their tails up its ass or other holes in place of wrapping around a nonexistent tail. There are a species of two-tailed cat people but, they are kind of rare these days. Many of them were killed in the Feudal Era of Japan during our first colonization attempt. However, there is at least one family we sent to earth that is still alive. Within that family is a boy about your age." Neko said, "Cool!" Eureka said, "Whatever you do, do not look for him he has reportedly succumbed to a corruption sealed away in the time of the first colonization attempt. If he sees you, he will likely attack and there is not a mortal alive that can kill him at this time." Eureka warned, "If you see an abandoned city, leave it immediately. Do not investigate it further or he may kill you! In the off-chance you see him, perhaps he will spare you. It is even more likely that you will survive, if you act like he is a hero for his deeds." Neko said, "Alright I'll keep that in mind, besides avoiding abandoned places is there anything else I should know?"

Eureka said, " Just that if things look bad as far as achieving peace, we may start drafting males to donate their sperm to keep our species going and we may end up aging them to a minimum age needed to hold a gun and walk properly. If nothing else, we'll need to keep our population up. So, if a pretty cat girl needs a little company because her husband died to knock yourself out, Tiger." She gave him an unamused look after saying that last part.

Neko said, "Alright." Eureka said, "Oh one last thing that Roswell incident way back when. That was when we sent your family to earth and the family of the two-tailed one I told you to avoid. Basically, any time there was ever an incident involving an alien or animal demon life form it was probably one of us or another hybrid species." Commander Kick Your Ass said, "We are counting on you Neko, and if you can impress us with how you handle the peace process and rescuing our people on earth, we may let you be our King."

Meanwhile back on earth Wolfenstein Von Bark Bark was with K9 in the Neko Cola factory. Ruff Ruff said, "Hey dad since cat people gave us back to you two and well we returned their hostages, does this mean our species are friends now?" Wolfenstein Von Bark Bark said, "No! That was merely a prisoner exchange among parents, it means nothing to the larger war at hand. However, the addition of these meddlesome humans does pose a minor complication in our plans."

K 9 said, "Indeed! We thought the cat people were our greatest enemy but, if we don't watch ourselves the humans could take their place." Wolfenstein Von Bark Bark said, "We still have prisoners here prisoners of war. These people killed some our own, mostly soldiers of course but, even a civilians who threw rocks at them were met with death. Neko was not raised by his own people and thus knows not the brutality they showed. These prisoners of war deserve no special treatment rather, they need a taste of their own medicine." K 10 said, "I don't know about this, we were so close to getting a peace treaty and now you are going to do the one thing that may yet seal our fate?"

K 9 said, "K 10 don't be going soft on me, the humans may be more xenophobic than them but, they killed my parents they have to die! If we don't do this, our race cannot be avenged!" Sena was recording this entire conversation on a hidden video camera.

The camera was broadcasting the video live throughout the galaxy. It was being broadcast over the emergency feeds. Wolfenstein Von Bark Bark said, "Mine were tortured to death right in front of my eyes I was just a child!" Wolfenstein Von Bark Bark pulled the switch and families of men, women, and children who were cat people were put onto a conveyor belt. Neko was watching his space ship emergency feed in horror as he hurried back to Earth.

Some robotic hands with white 4 fingered gloves picked up the Cat people on the Conveyer Belt and began squeezing the shit out of them for fertilizer bins, the blood out of them for Neko cola, and the remains got thrown in the meat grinder to make dog food under the label, "Dog's Delight." The Neko cola label read, "Club Soda for Vampires." The Neko blood got fizz added to it and canned and bottled appropriately.

Wolfenstein Von Bark Bark and K9, put a can of the dog food on a plate and poured the Neko blood soda like it was wine into glasses and ate it together. Billions of viewers could only watch this in horror. Even their own citizens thought this was barbaric and completely above and beyond what is acceptable. Boycotts of these products began throughout the galaxy. Even on planets with vampires on it because, of the cruel practice when they could just have just used a syringe to get blood with less pain. They would still get the nutrient-rich blood they needed that way.

K 10 said, "D-Daddy I don't know you anymore this is madness!" Ruff Ruff said, "Dad! I understand you are upset with what they did to your parents but, this is just too much. How can you sleep at night as many more are watching their family members be put to death and worse still, eaten like this?!" The two of them left the factory in shame as Neko landed next to it.

K10 said, "Hi Neko the ones you want inside have at them anyone who'd do what they are doing deserves to die." Ruff Ruff said, "I agree, war or not this is too much. Honestly I think peace is too much to hope for after what they've done." Neko nodded and ran inside the factory. There he saw that the broadcast wasn't fake at all. He shot the guards and factory workers inside and threw and Arclight Spanner into the machine to jam it as he freed the other captive Nekos.

The captive Neko's got away and Neko tried to leave but, was cornered. Wolfenstein Von Bark Bark asked, "Going somewhere Neko?" Neko said, "I was a fool to think maybe you weren't so terrible. I am sorry I didn't kill you sooner but, alas better late than never." Neko continued, "While I was rescuing the hostages, I planted C4 all over this entire building, particularly in the gas tanks. You aren't going anywhere." Sena jumped in from where she was secretly filming them and shot a rope gun at them. They were tied up with a rope made of some of the toughest coils around.

Neko put them into the room where the main valves the gas pipeline were housed. He grabbed a flamethrower and welded the door to that room shut trapping the two canines hybrids inside. He then ran out the front door with Sena, closed the door and welded it shut. Neko then, activated the C4 which caused a massive action movie style explosion behind them. It would be impossible for one to survive it, unless they somehow had explosion proof armor from head to toe. The two hybrids that were trapped inside did not have explosion proof armor.

Cheers erupted on all the hybrid planets in the galaxy. Ruff Ruff succeeded his father on Canis Major and K10 succeeded his father on Canis Minor. The following day Neko got together with both planet leaders and signed a peace treaty. Neko was Planet Neko's First King and Sena was their first Queen. Nekki Qui was made Head of The various forms of armed forces both cat hybrid and machine although most of the commanding of the vital forces was managed by Commander Kick Your Ass while, Nekki Qui oversaw the building and security of the mechanical forces. Sena gave birth to a beautiful baby girl whom they named Serena.

14 NICE TO MATE WITH YOUR ACQUAINTANCE
The Pleasure is all mine!

In the wake of this new era of peace for the hybrids on their
planets, the mating season was underway. Earth still remained a
hybrid risk zone as there were still yet threats there but, none were of
the immediate concern to Planet Neko. Despite this, there wasn't a
single cat person alive that didn't know that even when all seems well,
war can happen anytime. Throughout the entire conflict thousands of
soldiers on all sides of the war had died in just that year alone. As
such, all parties needed to do their own repopulating. Ruff Ruff and
K10 oversaw their own people's season and even helped where they
could.

To keep diplomatic relations warm, Planet Canis Major sent a
prospective female to mate with a potential cat male. The thinking
was that by interspecies breeding, perhaps peace could last at least
among their races. Until that day it had been a taboo or unheard of.
The female's name was Acela. The male chosen by the Nekos' name
was Nicholas. Both were a little nervous as for them it was their first
time and they'd never dealt with a being of another species.

Neko took them to a place called Lover's Lake where couples
fall in love and the bitterest of enemies consequently get
overwhelmed by their own hatred. Nekki Qui although not part of
this deal, was also at the lake with a cat girl that had purple hair pink
eyes and was probably the strongest female cat person on the planet.
Her name was Ayla.

Nicholas blushed and looked at Acela. Nicholas said, "Hi I am
Nicholas nice to mate, I mean meet you!" He covered his head
expecting to get hit for the horrible joke. Acela blushed and laughed
and said, "Hi I am Acela and are your parents ok with us doing this?"
Nicholas said, "Mine died in the Neko Cola factory... I was there."
He broke into tears. Acela said, "I-I am sorry..." She continued in
tears, "Mine died when the Nekos invaded our planet and my parents
threw rocks at them."

Both Nicholas and Acela, held each other tightly. Nicholas
wrapped his tail around Acela and Acela licked and sucked on his
ears. Acela pulled away slightly and unstrapped her multiple nipple
bra from the front, the straps made of Velcro and making a sort of
tearing sound as she took it off.

Acela rubbed all six of her nipples against his male nipples and tummy. She had a C cup for each nipple and both Acela and Nicholas appeared to be about 16. Nicholas pulled out a 10-inch penis barbed like a cat's. Nicholas was naked prior this encounter except for a loincloth on his penis. Nicholas curiously groped her breasts starting with the ones on top to the ones on the bottom.

This sent a wave of pleasure throughout Acela, as she stared with her aqua blue eyes into the hazel eyes of Nicholas. Her brown hair and fur swayed with the occasional gusts of wind as did the green hair Nicholas sported. Both of them sported Hippie Style hair in the sense that it was relatively long and unkempt.

Acela picked up Nicholas and slid his unusually large cat penis between her bottom and middle breasts while, letting him suck on her top two breasts like a baby trying to get milk. Nicholas let out the cutest moans as her breasts constricted his 10-inch long penis and Acela moaned cutely in response to him sucking on her nipples. Her claws dug into his back as he continued relentlessly and she was dripping out of her naked vaginal slit.

By this point, Nekki Qui was following along with the other two at the lake, except Ayla dominated Nekki Qui. She was straddling on his barbed kitty penis in a cowgirl position while, Nicholas was in a cowboy position dominating Acela. Acela said, "N-Nicholas… You feel so great in me!" She yelped in pleasure from his barbed kitty penis and howled.

Ayla had eight nipples and they were about the same size as Acela's, despite the fact she and Nekki Qui were about 6 years old at this point. Ayla said, "You make good sex Mr. Qui." Nekki Qui said, "You are so tight, I wonder why no one or hardly anyone has been down here. I'd think all the boys would want some of this!" Ayla said, "Strong men don't like Ayla, they are too puny for Ayla and it threatens them." Nekki Qui said, "Well at this rate, I won't walk properly for a long time!" Ayla said sternly, "Deal with it Man-bitch! Your spawn had better be more skilled at sex than you to his girlfriend or her boyfriend when he or she grows up, or I will make you pay big time."

Ayla continued straddling Nekki Qui letting out an enormous moan, as her hymen burst and she orgasmed all over Nekki Qui. Nekki Qui unleashed his sperm from his 10-inch penis exchanging moans of pleasure with her. He felt like a toothpick went through his kitty penis.

Nicholas' Ten-inch penis continued penetrating Acela. Acela said, "Nicholas it's too big!" Her hymen burst and with that, she orgasmed letting out howls of pain and pleasure. Nicholas unleashed his sperm as she did.

Once the two couples finished their mating, Neko began donating his sperm the "hard" way to any females he could find. This way they could get new sons and daughters. Neko agreed to help them as best as one could to take care of the young. Because he couldn't realistically be a good father to everyone on the planet, he gave priority to females of infertile males. Sena agreed to Surrogate for any infertile women on their behalf. Neko had invented a pill that could make births instant and even extract the baby safely.

Before long, the planet was full of kids from both Neko and Sena. About 1/3 of all children would be genetically linked to Neko, and 1/3 to Sena. Neko, Sena, and the Animal Hybrids of Planet Neko and beyond lived Sexually Ever After!

THE END!

ABOUT THE AUTHOR

Adam Thomas Applebaum has an Associate in Applied Sciences Degree in Computer Information Systems. His backstory is one only his trusted friends will ever know in full unless he publishes an Autobiography of it. He writes books like this one and tutors children in a variety of subjects, if the kids are High school level and below.

Please Contact Me

Phone: 310-561-6330

Email: adam.applebaum1@gmail.com

Or

Add me on Facebook

https://www.facebook.com/adam.applebaum1

To further support my Efforts

Author Website:

http://www.adamthomasapplebaum.com/

Subscribe to Me on YouTube:

http://www.youtube.com/user/AdathorRules

Follow me on Blogger: http://adamgmail.blogspot.com/

www.ingramcontent.com/pod-product-compliance
Lightning Source LLC
Chambersburg PA
CBHW030534020726
47494CB00004B/1362